OPERATION

BLAZING SNOW

OPERATION
BLAZING SNOW

Varun Bhakay

PARTRIDGE

To order additional copies of this book, contact
Partridge India
000 800 10062 62
orders.india@partridgepublishing.com

www.partridgepublishing.com/india

CONTENTS

Chapter 1   The Operation and the Operative 1
Chapter 2   Battleground Surveillance 10
Chapter 3   Political Monkeying, The Exodus and the Separatist Call 17
Chapter 4   Massacre or Self-Defence:
             The Evening of January 21st 1990 27
Chapter 5   Friction between Factions 32
Chapter 6   Turbulence: Meeting on the Nagin Lake 38
Chapter 7   A Plan 49
Chapter 8   The Escapade 54
Chapter 9   The Muzaffarabad Masterstroke 59
Chapter 10   Brass at Raisina Hill 75
Chapter 11   Revelations 93
Chapter 12   Mystery 97
Chapter 13   Turning the Tide 106
Chapter 14   Maulana's Provocation 115
Chapter 15   Action 119
Chapter 16   Meeting Foes 130
Chapter 17   The Fallen 139
Chapter 18   Boom! 151
Chapter 19   The Final Act 157

To Mamma and Papa

INTRODUCTION

Thank you for picking up Operation Blazing Snow. First up, I'd like to clarify that this is not a story about Kashmir. It's a story set in Kashmir. The Kashmir of 1990. Certain historical events of the time have been re-created and, in some cases, slightly modified to suit the storyline. No part of the story is intended to hurt anyone and I apologise in case anyone is offended by any part of it. I request the reader to treat the story as a work of fiction and as a means of entertainment.

It was around a year back, on January 15th 2015, that the idea of writing this story came to me. That night, I created three characters and the outline of the story under the tentative title 'The Kashmir Furnace'. Three months later, in April 2015, free from the burden of examinations, I started to write. I simultaneously read up a lot about the situation in the Valley twenty-five years ago. I quizzed people who had first-hand experience of the situation of the time. Armed with as much detail as I could handle, I finished my first draft on January 27th 2016, in 289 days.

Kashmir is the most beautiful place I've visited in my sixteen years of existence. I have spent a total of forty-four months in the northern-most state of India. My father often repeats the famed verse by Amir Khusrow about Kashmir: *"Agar firdaus bar ru-ye zamin ast, Hamin ast-o hamin ast-o hamin ast."* These lines, when translated into English, mean: "If there is a paradise on earth, It is this, it is this, it is this." For me, Kashmir is the closest one can possibly get to the concept of paradise: Srinagar with its Dal Lake, Shalimar and Nishat Baghs, Chashme Shahi, Chaar Chinar, Floating Market and Tulip Garden; Banihal (in Jammu Division) with that engineering marvel called the Jawahar Tunnel, which links Jammu Division and Kashmir Division; Verinag; Pampore, which is well-known for its saffron; the Wular Lake, Asia's largest wetland; Gulmarg; Pahalgam; and of course, Ladakh. I have also seen the other

Kashmir. The one you will read about in the story. The Kashmir of uniforms, vehicles, weapons and barbed wire.

All I can say now is sit back, turn the page and let me take you back twenty six years!

Varun Bhakay
February 15th 2016
Pune

ABBREVIATIONS

JAKRIF   : Jammu and Kashmir Rifles
NSG   : National Security Guard
LFTE   : Liberation Forces of Tamil Eelam
R&AW   : Research and Analysis Wing
K2   : Kashmir and Khalistan
KGB   : Komitet Gosudarstvennoy Bezopasnosti-Committee for State Security
IPS   : Indian Police Service
CIA   : Central Intelligence Agency
FBI   : Federal Bureau of Investigation
ISI   : Inter-Services Intelligence Directorate
FLJK   : Front for Liberation of Jammu and Kashmir
HM   : Hizbul Mujahideen
PsW/PW   : Prisoners of War/Prisoner of War
AKF   : Azad Kashmir Fauj
LC   : Line of Control
JKP   : Jammu and Kashmir Police
GBC   : Global Banking Corporation
IAF   : Indian Air Force
HSC   : Higher Secondary Certificate
BSF   : Border Security Force
CRPF   : Central Reserve Police Force
ASN   : Army Satellite Network
GOC   : General Officer Commanding
MLA   : Member of Legislative Assembly
KPs   : Kashmiri Pandits

PM   : Prime Minister
PMO   : Prime Minister's Office
SLRs   : Self-Loading Rifles
JCO   : Junior Commissioned Officer
NCO/NCOs   : Non-Commissioned Officer/Non-Commissioned Officers
DSP   : Deputy Superintendent of Police
PRO   : Press Relations Officer
AIR   : All India Radio
IB   : Intelligence Bureau
MARCOs   : Marine Commandos
JAKLI   : Jammu and Kashmir Light Infantry
SAG   : Special Action Group
ADG   : Additional Director General
NSD   : National School of Drama
SFF   : Special Frontier Force
2IC   : Second-in-Command
RPG   : Rocket-Propelled Grenade
ECCE   : Extreme Cold Climate Equipment
LAC   : Line of Actual Control
IMA   : Indian Military Academy
CGO   : Central Government Offices
ISD   : International Subscriber Dialling
AFSPA   : Armed Forces Special Powers Act
SP   : Superintendent of Police
PoK   : Pakistan-occupied Kashmir
IARDC   : Indian Atomic Research & Development Centre
ED   : Enforcement Directorate
CBI   : Central Bureau of Investigation
SOG   : Special Operations Group
CI   : Counter-Insurgency
CO   : Commanding Officer
IEDs   : Improvised Explosive Devices

PROLOGUE

In other towns, one of the most deadly events in Kashmir's history had unfolded rapidly. Earlier in the day, people had emerged on to the streets in enormous numbers. *"People's League ka kya hai paigham? Fateh, Azadi aur Islam!"*, *"Kashmir mein agar rehna hai, Allah-ho-Akbar kehna hai!"*, *"Dil mein rakho Khuda ka khauf, Haath mein Kalashnikov!"*, *"Pakistan Zindabad, Hindustan Murdabad!"* Shouting these slogans, men holding aloft banners which said 'FLJK', 'Hizbul' and 'Azadi' walked through streets of towns across the Valley. Some of them carried that dreaded Russian assault rifle, the Kalashnikov while others carried the flag of Pakistan. They were joined by many more people along their march, mostly enthusiastic youngsters. Kashmir's government was already in tatters and was unwilling to act against the Separatists. New Delhi refused to give the Army and other security forces permission to intervene and bring the situation under control. The Kashmiri Pandits, or KPs, were rendered helpless. They huddled together in large numbers, praying fervently for a miracle. The Hizbul Mujahideen had issued an ultimatum, demanding that the Pandits either leave the Valley or face dire consequences. The threat to their lives had been growing day-by-day for nearly a month. Some families packed up their belongings and hurried away to Jammu. A majority of the KPs were unwilling to leave their homes. "We belong here as much as the Muslims!" declared MLA Umesh Pandita in a public rally in Srinagar moments before he was shot dead. The situation spiralled out of control, beginning with kidnappings and growing to murders. Pandits stopped stepping out of their houses but things didn't improve. That evening, incited by radicals and militant leaders, fanatics entered the towns of Sopore, Anantnag, Baramulla, Bandipora, Shopian, Awantipora, Tral, Pampore, Handwara, Kupwara, Handwara and Pulwama and painted crosses and wrote their names on houses of Pandits. Similar incidents occurred across other towns. More Pandits left the Valley in clutches, clogging the Jawahar Tunnel at Banihal as darkness descended like a bat. Kalashnikov-wielding men entered houses that had not been vacated. The occupants were thrashed within an inch of their lives. Women and children were brutally raped by the militants. Men were forced to watch as their families underwent harrowing torture. The militants plundered all they could from the houses and the people. They then either mowed the families down with bullets or set the houses on fire with the occupants inside, alive and breathing. The fires all over the Valley symbolised the overall scenario: Kashmir was burning. The fire was spreading and desperate measures were needed to bring it under control.

**

1

THE OPERATION AND THE OPERATIVE

A tall man with fair features, dark hair, piercing gun-metal grey eyes and a beard got off the local train at Chanakyapuri. The ride had been a lonely one but Major Liaquat Khaleel Baig preferred it that way. He looked around the platform but saw no one apart from a few tea vendors. They all seemed engrossed in their own work and nobody was bothered about the almost empty train that had just arrived. Not a single vehicle was on the roads on the cold January morning. Delhiites preferred staying indoors until the sun was shining.

Born in Bijbehara, Kashmir, Baig had joined the Indian Army ten years back, in 1980. He had been commissioned into the Jammu and Kashmir Rifles and had served in his battalion for five years before going to the National Security Guard, India's 'Black Cat' commando establishment, on a two-year attachment. He had done a commendable job and had even participated in classified operations in Sri Lanka against the rebel guerrilla force Liberation Forces of Tamil Eelam. His work was spotted by an Additional Director in the Research & Analysis Wing. He was subsequently deputed to India's premier espionage agency for a stint of three years. The R&AW had been around for nineteen years by then. He had been sent on an undercover assignment to Pakistan and had managed to join their Army under a false identity and served in it for two years before he was betrayed by a fellow agent who had turned traitor. He had managed to kill the traitor and had escaped. He had returned just a few weeks back. His deputation with the R&AW was

1

about to come to an end and he had already decided that he was not going to ask for an extension. He felt that some of his worst nightmares had been better than his time at the R&AW.

From Chanakyapuri, he took an auto-rickshaw to South Block and arrived well in time for his meeting. Here, not a single minister of the brand new Yashvardhan Sahni-government seemed to have arrived. He was led into the office of Secretary (Research), Nikhil Thapar, the Head of the R&AW. Thapar was a legendary character. In thirty years of service, he had done some hair-raising work. As a Field Agent, he had been sent to Pakistan and had joined their Army. He served in it for five years and passed information about Zia-ul-Haq's K2 plans. Upon his return, he had been involved in gathering intelligence from India's allies. He had then held negotiations with Naxals in Central India before being chosen to head the Intelligence Bureau. After a year in the Bureau, he was promoted to Secretary (Research). He was supposedly close to many top KGB agents and many Opposition leaders had alleged that he routinely passed information to them. He walked in a couple of minutes after Baig's arrival, accompanied by Director of Covert Operations (Pakistan) Samir Ali.

"'Morning, Liaquat," said Thapar.

"'Morning, sir!' said Baig.

"Turned out to be quite the slippery snake in Pakistan, Liaquat," said Samir and gave Baig a hug.

The two had known each other for a very long time. Samir and Baig's elder brother Mudassar had been classmates in school and college. Both had joined the IPS together and after Mudassar's death in an encounter with Maoists in Bihar, Samir had taken Liaquat under his wing.

"How was Pakistan?" asked Thapar.

"Picturesque, sir. I saw a lot of places and a lot of stuff. That cricket kid Sachin Tendulkar. Saw him at Peshawar. He pulled Abdul Qadir to pieces."

"What else did you see?" asked Ali.

"AK-47s. By the truck-load. Pakistan are smuggling them over from the Soviet Union. And a lot of other automatic weapons from the States. They've got guys in both countries who are hand-in-glove with corrupt politicians and bureaucrats as well as the Mafia. All the other details are in here," Baig slid a file over to Thapar.

"Samir, tell Mishra to get his boys in Russia moving. Tanya should be told to put a few KGB agents on the job once we are done here. I want Mathews to talk to the CIA or the FBI too. Have a look," said Thapar.

"Right!"

Despite the fact that Ali's job entailed overlooking covert operations in Pakistan, he was Thapar's right-hand man and was often deputed to carry out other tasks.

"Anything else, Liaquat?" asked Thapar.

"Pakistan has restarted its work in Kahuta. For quite some time, no activity related to nuclear missiles was being carried out. The ISI is going to be sending agents under a covert operation codenamed 'Tupac'."

"What about Raghubir?" quizzed Ali.

Baig looked around the office for a moment before answering.

"The amount of money he had been given was atrocious. As was his field work. He couldn't shadow anyone. He couldn't get people talking. But he talked. He talked as if it were his favourite hobby. Everything he knew, he told them! Of course, he didn't know anything that could be considered significant. I had bugged his clothes, so I knew when the police would come knocking on my door. I went to his place and waited for him. Shot him as soon as he entered. He bled out in seconds."

"What did you do, empty the clip?" asked Ali.

"No," said Baig plainly. "Two!"

Neither Thapar nor Ali looked the least bit surprised. Baig had a notorious habit of going beyond his brief.

"And so, I went to Wagah along with a bunch of pilgrims who were headed to Amritsar. Just joined the lot with a turban on my head. Credit to Sam. Before I left, he gave me a fake ID according to which I was a Sikh. I thought it was worthless. He didn't. From Amritsar, I came to Delhi. Been here for two weeks."

"Raghubir was dead?" asked Thapar.

"Yes. One hundred percent."

"All right then. That's one more asshole out of the way! Let's get down to business. Liaquat, what do you know about the situation in Kashmir?" said Thapar.

"Militancy is on the rise. It has always been existent in the state but after the death of Sheikh Ahmed and the tussle for power between Farhad Ahmed and his brother-in-law, it has grown in massive numbers. Politics can be blamed for all of it. When the First Kashmir War was still on, our then Prime Minister dragged the issue to the UN. That was one of our biggest blunders as an independent country because Pakistan refused to vacate the territory they had occupied and a plebiscite, which had been promised, was never held. In 1965, we captured the Haji Pir Pass, which cut short the distance from Jammu, through Poonch, to Srinagar and the rest of the Valley. In the 1966 Tashkent Agreement, it was returned to Pakistan. Since then, Pakistan has been sending infiltrators into Kashmir through the Pass as well. In the current scheme of things, the two main terror outfits in the Valley are the Front for Liberation of Jammu and Kashmir, also known as the FLJK, and the Hizbul Mujahideen. In 1984, an Indian diplomat, Rajiv Phadnis, was killed in Birmingham by the FLJK. They had wanted their leader, Manzoor Butt, to be released. When their demands weren't met, Phadnis was murdered in cold blood. In return, Butt was hanged in Tihar Jail five days later. Things took a big turn and went from bad to worse in 1987. The year of that notorious Assembly Election. Soon after Farhad Ahmed 'won' the election, young boys were recruited and sent for training to Pakistan. That was the beginning of the militancy on a large scale. Currently, the Separatists are trying to organise a militant uprising under that senile fool Syed Mohammed Ali Hussain. They kidnapped Home Minister Maqsood Shahid's daughter in December last year and had demanded that five of their comrades be freed. Those men were released and the girl was returned safe and sound. Maulana Omar Faisal of the Moderates has desperately tried to diffuse the tension by suggesting talks but they aren't materialising at all. And Article 370 isn't really helping matters. If you ask me, had we bargained for all of Kashmir after '71 in exchange for Pakistan's ninety-three thousand prisoners, the problem could have been solved. Instead, we returned their Prisoners of War along with ridiculous amounts of captured territory, didn't get all Indian Prisoners of War back in return and ended up looking like idiots," explained Baig.

"Well done on the homework quotient, Liaquat," smiled Thapar.

"It helps to stay in touch with events back home, sir," said Baig.

"We're calling this one Operation Blazing Snow. Your assignment is a rather complicated one, Liaquat. We need you to infiltrate a Separatist group in Kashmir."

"And which lucky group will have the honour of meeting me, sir?" asked Baig, picking up a glass of water.

"The militant wing of the FLJK: the Azad Kashmir Fauj," said Ali.

"What will be my cover story?" asked Baig.

"You'll be an officer of the Pakistan Army sent to Kashmir by the ISI to turn more boys into militants and to train them within the Valley itself," said Ali.

Baig immediately raised a red flag.

"Sir, what if they make a phone call to the ISI?"

"We recently captured an agent of theirs: a Major Zulfiqar Afridi from the Pakistan Army. He cracked under interrogation. We confiscated all the documents that he possessed. All the information and paperwork we have about him, including correspondence, will be handed over to you. Also, news of his capture has not spread because nothing has been released to the press and we are also monitoring all international calls to and from Kashmir. Only the Prime Minister knows that we have captured an ISI agent. Others believe we are still pursuing him. The Intelligence Bureau has released a statement that an ISI agent has entered India and efforts are being made to capture him. Hopefully, that will keep Pakistan under the impression that their chap is up and about. Also, the border crossings have reduced since the Army beefed up their strength along the LC," explained Thapar.

"So I impersonate him and infiltrate the FLJK?" asked Baig.

"Yes. Colonel Vikrant Pratap of the Corps Headquarters is your main contact in Srinagar. Keep him informed of any militant activity you hear about. You'll find his number, along with a few other important ones in the documents," said Thapar.

"You will be taken to Srinagar from where another operative, Inspector Sajid Wali Lone of the Jammu and Kashmir Police, who has already joined the FLJK, will assist you in this operation. In case you need to get in touch with anyone, Lone has been given a Motorola satellite phone which cannot be tracked or tapped. Its encryption is too complicated so make sure you don't use a scrambler set. And there are a few more fake identity cards for you and Lone," said Ali and handed Baig a heavy file with the words 'OPERATION BLAZING SNOW' neatly written in red across its front.

"Liaquat, this is more or less a trial operation. You have to be extremely careful," said Thapar.

"Excuse me, sir?"

"It's the first of its kind. The Wing will mount more operations like this one if the trial is successful."

"So this policeman and I are the Wing's guinea pigs?"

"I suppose you could say that."

"What about my weapon?"

"Saxena, the Head of Armoury, will meet you outside the airport with that," said Thapar.

"Do I get a choice or something?"

"No! Saxena feels that you do your best to destroy anything fancy. Hence, you'll be getting a standard-issue Walther P1," said Ali.

"Bloody clot of a chap, that Saxena!"

"I hope you won't talk like that about him to his face. Knowing Saxena, he'll end up giving one of those wooden swords in shiny paper. The kind you get during Dussehra," Ali remarked.

"Ha-ha! Sam, your joke was so funny that I forgot to laugh. Anyway, I'll take your leave, sir."

"All the best, Liaquat!" Thapar clapped Baig on the back.

"Thank you, sir."

"Good luck, kiddo!" said Ali.

"Thanks, grandpa!"

Sometime later, Baig picked up his stuff from a flat he had taken on rent, ate breakfast at a roadside stall and from there, he went to meet his sister Shehnaaz in Vasant Kunj.

"How are you doing, Liaquat?" she asked when they had settled into her drawing room.

"Pretty good. Deputation's almost over,"

"You've applied for an extension?"

"Nope. I'm tired. I want to go back to riding my Bullet and being around the men and the officers. What I've learnt in my time with the

R&AW is to never take films seriously. James Bond is a lie! Never been to an exotic location or driven an exotic car!"

"Or slept with a beautiful woman!" Shehnaaz smirked.

"Remind me what your loser of a husband looks like again?" Baig retorted.

"So where is your next assignment?" Shehnaaz hurriedly changed the subject.

"They want me to go home."

"What's it about?"

"Aha! If I told you that, I'd have to kill you."

"Going to meet *Ammi* and *Abbu*?"

"No. And you'd better not tell them anything. They can't deal with such stuff anymore."

"Okay."

"What's up with you?"

"I'm being promoted to Head of Department for English at the university," Shehnaaz's tone was one of exasperation.

"You don't sound to be too happy about it."

"I'm not. I don't want to be a Head of Department. I won't be able to teach anymore if I accept the appointment."

"Isn't that good? Who wants to be around those monkeys, or students as you call them, all day?!"

"I do. Teaching is a passion for me, Liaquat."

"Spare me your sermons, Shehnaaz. How's Randeep?"

"He's fine. He's gone to New York for a series of meetings."

"Again? Seriously, his job isn't so great that he has to have meetings constantly! That too abroad," said Baig hotly.

Baig's brother-in-law and Shehnaaz's husband Randeep Singh was the Managing Director of Global Banking Corporation's Indian Subcontinent division. He often disappeared on long tours, which made Baig wonder what exactly he was up to and made him worried for Shehnaaz. Baig had been against his sister marrying Randeep but hadn't voiced his misgivings to anyone but his brother Mudassar. Mudassar too didn't want Shehnaaz to marry Randeep but wished for his parents and sister to be happy. As he told Baig, "As long as Shehnaaz has no objections, why should it bother us?"

"Liaquat, I know you don't like him but please relax!"

"Fine! I just wish you'd told me why you wanted to marry that ass in the first place! What is the nature of his meetings anyway?"

"He says that it's 'confidential'."

"Yeah right! Typical of that cowardly bastard! He can never give a straight answer. Anyway, screw him! I'm leaving Samir Ali's number here. Call him if you need to get in touch with me. But only if it's something urgent."

"The same Samir who was Mudassar's best friend?"

"The very same. Take care then. And remember, not a word to either *Ammi-Abbu* or that idiot husband of yours!"

"Bye. And Liaquat, try not to get hurt."

Baig winked at his sister and ran down the stairs. He walked to the main road and spotted a telephone booth there. He dialled the R&AW extension and was patched to Samir Ali within seconds.

"Hi, Sam! Can you do me a favour?"

"Yeah, tell me."

"Can you get one of our American assets to tail Shehnaaz's husband Randeep?"

"Why? What's wrong? Liaquat, the Wing isn't going to waste resources based on your personal opinion of your brother-in-law."

"Just get it done, Sam. I want to know everything. Whom he meets, where he meets them, where he is staying and most importantly, what is he up to in New York City!"

"I'll look into it."

"Thanks."

"Good luck for Blazing Snow, Liaquat."

"Thanks!"

Baig took a taxi to the airport. He was looking around the terminal entrance for Saxena when he felt a tap on his shoulder.

"Major Baig," said the Head of the R&AW Armoury.

"Mister Saxena. Good Morning."

"I've got your weapon," he handed Baig a small case.

"Thank you. How many extra magazines?"

"Nine."

"Cool. I'd better get going then. Thanks again."

"Bye, Major."

At half-past twelve, Baig boarded an Antonov An-12 aircraft of the Indian Air Force for Srinagar. As he saw the national capital disappear under the clouds, he wondered whether he'd ever see it again. Then he settled down and took out Frederick Forsyth's The Day of the Jackal. He got goosebumps as Lieutenant Colonel Bastien-Thierry's men opened fire on President General Charles de Gaulle's car.

**

2
BATTLEGROUND SURVEILLANCE

At 1500 hours on the afternoon of January 18ᵗʰ 1990, the Indian Air Force Antonov An-12 aircraft carrying Major Liaquat Baig of the Research and Analysis Wing and eleven personnel of the Indian Army touched down at Srinagar Air Force Station, which also doubled as the civilian airport. Baig noticed a tall, robust man in the Arrivals lounge. He was holding a board which said 'ZULFIQAR AFRIDI'. He nodded at the man who walked up to him and introduced himself in a whisper.

"Major Liaquat Baig? Sir, I am Inspector Sajid Wali Lone of the Jammu and Kashmir Police. I will be assisting you in our work here."

"What is the current scenario looking like, Sajid?" asked Baig.

"Not good at all, sir. The new Governor is expected to take charge in a couple of days and the locals, rather those who support the Separatists, are still attempting to organise a mass-agitation," replied Lone as walked towards a white Maruti 800.

"Where are we going to be staying?" asked Baig.

"Downtown," said Lone as he accelerated.

"Where are you from?"

"My parents fled Muzaffarabad during the first war with Pakistan. My father managed to buy an apple orchard in Sopore and they settled down over there. I was born in Sopore and grew up there. What about you, sir?"

"Bijbehara. My father was in the Army, my brother in the IPS."

"Nice. So your motivation to join the Forces must have had a lot to do with being attached to the organisation, right?"

"Pretty much. What about you?"

"Sopore, as you must be aware, is the hotbed of militancy in India. The problem of militants always existed in Sopore, and that too in a larger number than the rest of the Valley. It was there when I was growing up and it was highly influential. There were fourteen of us in our HSC class. Ten joined militant organisations and the others were killed for refusing to take up arms. I joined the Kashmir Mujahideen, which was a fledging organisation at that time. I was taken to their base in Pattan."

"What?!" Baig had a horrified look on his face.

"Relax, sir. I was working for the J&K Police as an informer. I torched the KM base in my fourth week there. They lost all their men, arms, ammunition and of course, the base. They had just started off. The group was mainly made up of people who had left other outfits due to differences. And fortunately, they were based only in Pattan because other towns like Shopian, Baramulla, Manasbal, Anantnag and Pulwama were occupied by bigger groups. Of course, wiping out minnows like the KM was not a big achievement but other groups were certainly taken aback!"

"Wow! That's pretty good."

As they drove down the almost empty roads, Baig saw the sidewalks swarming with security forces personnel. Sandbag bunkers and barbed wire were in abundance and the few locals on the street looked cautious and somewhat scared. Lone needed to collect a parcel for the FLJK on Gupkar Road. They drove down it, looking at the posh bungalows occupied by senior bureaucrats and politicians, apart from a magnificent golf course. They drove on until they reached what looked like the end of the road. A man stood near a Premier Padmini with a huge sack on the bonnet. Lone stopped a few yards ahead and got out. The man took four thousand rupee notes from Lone, who pulled a metal box out of the sack and took out something shiny. The two men shook hands. Lone heaved the sack back to the 800 and shoved it at the bottom of the backseat, sliding across a panel at the base of the seat and pushing the sack into the secret compartment.

"Ammunition for Kalashnikovs. AK-47s. He is from Kupwara. Helps in collecting weapons in the forest there," explained Lone as he took a u-turn.

As they drove ahead, Baig noticed a roadblock. It was manned by men from the Border Security Force and was at the gates of a huge bungalow. The place had an eerie look to it. Through the fencing, they saw that it was swarming with BSF men and officers. Lone slowed down the speed of the 800 considerably.

"Papa 2," he whispered to Baig.

Papa 2 was a detention centre under the BSF. Kashmiri boys and men who were suspected of militant and anti-national activities were imprisoned there. It functioned from the beginning of the insurgency up to the mid-90s. Locals shuddered when the place was mentioned. The BSF had been accused of carrying out brutal atrocities in order to get the detainees to tell the truth. The allegations were never proved in a court of law. Many other detention centres also existed, with names akin to something constructed and christened by a mad scientist: Harinawas, Cargo, Gogoland, a theatre called Shiraz Cinema. Allegedly, atrocities similar to the ones of Papa 2 were carried out in the other centres as well and like Papa 2, the charges were never proved.

"Open the boot," said a BSF soldier who came to check the 800's papers as three others surrounded the car with their rifles pointing at it.

Lone did as he was told. The soldiers checked each bit of the car. They didn't notice the switch for the panel at the base of the backseat.

"ID?" said the leader.

"Here," said Lone, handing a card.

"Jan Mohammed?"

"Yes, sir. I am with Khabr-e-Kashmir. I am writing an article on the BSF right now. About the good work they have done in the Valley. At our newspaper, we believe in supporting the security forces," Lone spoke in a voice that clearly indicated that he was sucking up to the soldier.

"Okay. You can go."

They drove past colourful shops, restaurants and emporiums on the posh Residency Road which was swarming with people. The bunkers of the Central Reserve Police Force were the only things that looked out of place. Lal Chowk-the business hub of Srinagar. Traders and shopkeepers make booming profits from the tourists who visit the Valley. It is also notorious for its strong anti-India sentiments. The atmosphere there is always tense. Things can go from peaceful to violent in a matter of minutes. Lal Chowk contributes heavily to the unpredictability of the Valley. Baig noticed an abnormally large number of Pakistani flags fluttering here and there. The Ghanta Ghar which had been erected by the motor giant Bajaj in the 80s appeared. Lately, it had been the face of numerous political rallies. Lone parked in a narrow lane and took out the bulging sack. They couldn't be seen by the CRPF men near the Ghanta Ghar anymore. Baig took his rucksack and followed Lone. The lane was empty but there were houses everywhere. They walked for around five minutes before Baig spotted a man with a Kalashnikov. He stopped them.

"Sajid, is that you? Who is he?"

"The fellow from the ISI," replied Lone and they continued.

They stopped in front of a door and Lone knocked. The door was opened and they were ushered in. Lone thrust the sack into the arms of a man in a *pheran* and led Baig into the huge house. Four platforms had been put up on the edge of the plot where lookouts were positioned. They went up a flight of stairs and entered a room.

"Major Zulfiqar Afridi of the ISI," said Lone, addressing the four men in the room. "Major, this is Mir Omar Faisal. He is the deputy leader of the Moderates of the All Party Azad Kashmir Conference," Lone gestured towards the youngest-looking of the lot. "Yasir Meer, commander of the Ayub Battalion of the Azad Kashmir Fauj," Meer shook hands with Baig. "Syed Mohammed Ali Hussain *sahib* leads the Hardliners in the APAKC," Lone indicated towards an old man who was sipping *kahwa*. "And this is Farooq Malik, commander of the Zia Battalion of the Azad Kashmir Fauj," Malik too shook hands with Baig.

"So Major, what news do you bring us?" asked Hussain.

"The time is ripe for action. The government at Delhi is new and inexperienced. Yasir and his boys have already shown how vulnerable they are. But we must act at the earliest. I heard before leaving Muzaffarabad that the Indian bureaucrat Jagdeep will be taking over as Governor soon," briefed Baig.

"These Indians will keep sending infidels to govern Kashmir. When will they learn? *Hum chahte hain azadi!*" said Hussain.

"Hussain *sahib*, we have to counter these people in the only language they seem to understand: load, aim and fire!" said Meer.

"Yasir, I am sure many boys will follow the path you have shown. It is the path that will free us from the shackles of India. Major *sahib*, ISI chief Mushtaq has said that you will impart small arms and close combat training to the boys. *Inshallah*, they will take our fight right up to 7 RCR," said Malik.

"But let us try to acknowledge that we should keep up with our efforts on the political front, Hussain *sahib*," said Faisal.

"Of course. We must try and engage in talks with the Indian government. It is essential that they fulfil our demands for freedom. Otherwise they should get used to dead bodies of soldiers lying on the roads of Kashmir," Hussain sounded quite demented.

"Sajid, take Major *sahib* to his quarters. You will keep him company there," said Malik, glancing at his wristwatch.

"Yes. We should leave immediately. Curfew will be imposed soon," Lone pointed out.

Baig bade everyone goodbye and followed Lone through the narrow streets to the car.

"This is what the situation is like. Faisal is okay but the rest are a bunch of raving lunatics, especially Hussain. You heard the way he was talking. Meer's future though, doesn't look too bright," smiled Lone as they got into the 800.

"You're going to pass information about his location?" asked Baig.

"Yes. He is going to be travelling to Sopore tonight. I have already informed the Army. Teams from a Rashtriya Rifles battalion will be waiting for him near his hideout. We'll be in touch with them over satellite phone," said Lone as they stopped at a CRPF checkpoint. "Of course, Meer's arrest could stir up some trouble."

"That means that it is possible for protests to break out at any moment."

"Sir, that is a risk that has to be taken in today's Kashmir," Lone smiled wryly and stopped the car in the Maisuma-Gawakadal area.

They went into a small lane and got into another large house.

"Abdul will bring food in the evening and go back. We will have company tomorrow morning but only for a short while. The leaders of the FLJK expect you to chalk out a plan as to how boys can be trained to become suicide bombers and good shooters," said Lone as he unlocked the door.

They went and sat in the drawing room, discussing what sort of combat they could possible train the budding militants in. An hour later, there was a knock on the door.

"Who is it?" asked Lone as Baig took cover with a pistol in hand.

"Abdul," came a squeaky voice.

Lone opened the door and took a plastic bag, handed the boy a hundred rupee note and closed the door again.

"Sir, relax. It's food,"

Lone and Baig switched off the satellite phone provided by the FLJK and switched on the higher-end Motorola. Abdul had brought them spicy mutton and soft Kashmiri *naans*. They ate quickly, cleaned up and came back to the drawing room. Lone picked up the Motorola and dialled.

"Pattan Exchange. This is Inspector Sajid Wali Lone of Jammu and Kashmir Police. Please connect me to Captain Vatsal Chauhan on the ASN," he said.

"Connecting, sir. Please stay on the line," said the operator.

A few minutes later, the set crackled.

"Vatsal here," said a voice from the other end.

"This is Inspector Lone from Srinagar," said Lone.

"Hi, Lone. What's the intel?"

"Yasir Meer has left Srinagar and is expected to reach Sopore at around eleven o'clock. He has seven men with him and all of them are armed. The hideout is at the edge of Sopore town, on a lane off the road that leads to Botingoo, Watlab, Wular Lake and Bandipora. It's the only house in that lane. And take some more men. The compound is quite big."

"Okay. We have placed squads on strategic points at Pattan and Sangrama overlooking the highway. Based on your intel, we'll surround the house as well. We've got reserve teams waiting at Adipora and Watlab. Anything else?"

"Try and get Meer alive. We may be able to extract some information from him," said Lone.

"Obviously," said the Captain and the line went dead.

Lone tuned into the AIR Srinagar channel on the radio and hummed the Kashmiri folk songs that were being played. Baig had taken out 'The Day of the Jackal' and they spent two hours in silence. Baig could hear the rumbling of vehicles and went on to the terrace to take a look. He could see headlights belonging to vehicles of the security forces and the Army. He asked Lone about them.

"They patrol the city after dark to ensure there is no problem or suspicious activity. There are patrols all over Downtown. Any passer-by can be stopped and searched," the Inspector answered as he lit a cigarette.

Baig returned to the drawing room and just then, the Motorola beeped. Lone adjusted the signal and the voice of Captain Vatsal Chauhan came through.

"Lone, we've got him. We've got Meer. The rest of the men with him were killed. Once they were inside the house, we took out the four men who had been left as look-outs. We told Meer to surrender but those buggers opened fire on us through the windows. We stormed the place, killed all of Meer's companions and then disarmed him. We'll be moving him to a different location tonight and tomorrow he will be taken back to Srinagar."

"Congratulations on the success, Chauhan. *Jai Hind!*" said Lone.

"*Jai Hind!*"

Lone's face was flushed with happiness.

"Well done, Sajid," said Baig.

"Thank you, sir,"

"What time will those boys be arriving tomorrow?"

"Around ten thirty,"

"Right then. Good night," said Baig and he went up the stairs to his bedroom.

He lay down on his bed, staring at the ceiling and hearing the movement of the patrolling vehicles. He said a quick prayer, hoping that his task would not be ruined now that Yasir Meer had been captured. If only politicians thought the same way. Unknown to Baig, the next three days would only add to the arduousness of his job.

**

3

POLITICAL MONKEYING, THE EXODUS AND THE SEPARATIST CALL

JANUARY 19TH 1990
FLJK HIDEOUT, MAISUMA-GAWAKADAL
SRINAGAR, INDIA

Liaquat Baig's first morning as an undercover agent in the Valley of Kashmir was a very cold one. The temperatures had dipped and dark clouds were gathering up in the skies. He looked at his wristwatch and relaxed. It was just quarter to eight. He could hear bustling downstairs. He got ready as quickly as he could and went down. Lone was making tea.

"Good Morning, Sajid," said Baig.

"'Morning, sir," came the reply.

"What's the status?"

"I tried calling Malik but he isn't picking up the phone. I don't like calling Hussain because being the old codger that he is, he starts snapping. Faisal hardly ever picks up the satellite phone given to him by the FLJK."

"Doesn't trust them?"

"Not at all. His father is actual leader of the Moderates. Maulana Omar Faisal. He is very pro-India. He doesn't support the fact that the APAKC want to send the boys across the border but he also feels that the security forces shouldn't go out of their way to make life miserable for the locals. Says that Partition, Pakistan and politicians are the ones to blame for the flaming cauldron Kashmir is in today," explained Lone.

"What are the FLJK and APAKC people like?" asked Baig.

17

"The APAKC is divided into two factions: the Hardliners, led by Hussain and the Moderates, led by Maulana. There is a third group: the Non-Aligned, but it's not big enough to be considered a faction. Hussain is the current President of the APAKC and dominates the meetings. Crazy as he is, he is also intelligent and an excellent orator. The meetings have no real significance, since neither faction can agree with the other. The last meeting was held a week back."

"Did you attend it?"

"Yes."

"What were the main topics of discussion?"

"The Hardliners were talking about more vandalism and *naarebaazi* at Lal Chowk, apart from a rise in the number of boys being sent to Pakistan. They also discussed ethnic cleansing, amidst protests from the Moderates."

"Ethnic cleansing? Something like the Holocaust perpetrated by the Nazis?"

"Not as bad but something similar. Not in concept, but in ideology. The Hardliners wish to drive the Pandits out of the Valley and kill those who don't leave."

"So it was something like Kashmir's Wannsee. Did they mention any specific date? When are they going to do it?"

"As far as I recall, no. All they said was 'on the date mentioned in the December meeting'."

"Call Malik! Immediately! He'll know the date. We need to alert Corps Headquarters!"

Lone dialled Malik's number as quickly as he could.

"*Assalaam Waleiqum*, Malik *bhai*. Sajid speaking."

"*Waleiqum Assalaam*, Sajid."

"The Major and I were discussing the last meeting of the APAKC."

"But he wasn't there," Malik cut Lone off.

"I was telling him about it. He seems rather interested in the concept of ethnic cleansing. When are we carrying it out?"

"'We' aren't carrying it out, my friend. No. We have delegated the task to the Area Commanders of the Front. They'll carry it out. It will be done tonight. In any case, our brothers from Hizbul have been issuing warnings since December. I hope, for the sake of the Pandits, that they have already cleared out. Who knows what our boys may end up doing?" Malik laughed.

"That's true. I too hope that they have cleared out. Makes our work easier. *Khuda Hafiz*."

"*Khuda Hafiz*."

Lone kept the phone on the table and turned to Baig.

"Sir, it's going to happen tonight."

Baig ran up the stairs to his room and pulled the OPERATION BLAZING SNOW file out of his rucksack. He ran back down, grabbed the Motorola and dialled a number. It was picked up after five rings.

"This is Colonel Vikrant Pratap," said a soft voice.

"Sir, this is Major Liaquat Baig of the R&AW. I was told to contact you in case I needed help."

"What news do you have, Baig?"

"Sir, the Separatists and their supporters are planning to cleanse the Valley of Pandits."

"I am aware that a threat to the Pandit community has been growing for a while."

"No, sir! I meant that they're going to do it tonight."

"Tonight?"

"Yes, sir."

"I'll let the GOC know. Thanks, Baig."

"Good day, sir."

The FLJK people who were supposed to turn up never did and all Baig and Lone could mutter was 'bloody militants'. The murky morning turned into a dark evening. Abdul came and went. Baig and Lone passed their time playing cards. Neither of them paid a lot of attention to the game. The fate of the Pandits was playing on their minds.

In other towns, one of the most deadly events in Kashmir's history had unfolded rapidly. Earlier in the day, people had emerged on to the streets in enormous numbers. *"People's League ka kya hai paigham? Fateh, Azadi aur Islam!"*, *"Kashmir mein agar rehna hai, Allah-ho-Akbar kehna hai!"*, *"Dil mein rakho Khuda ka khauf, Haath mein Kalashnikov!"*, *"Pakistan Zindabad, Hindustan Murdabad!"* Shouting these slogans, men holding aloft banners which said 'FLJK', 'Hizbul' and 'Azadi' walked through streets of towns across the Valley. Some of them carried that dreaded Russian assault rifle, the Kalashnikov while others carried the flag of Pakistan. They were joined by many more people along their march, mostly enthusiastic youngsters. Kashmir's government was already in tatters and was unwilling to act against the Separatists. New Delhi refused to give the Army and other security forces permission to intervene and bring the situation under control. The Kashmiri Pandits, or KPs, were rendered helpless. They huddled together in large numbers, praying fervently for a miracle. The Hizbul Mujahideen had issued an ultimatum, demanding that the Pandits either leave the Valley or face dire consequences. The threat to their lives had been growing day-by-day for nearly a month. Some families packed up their belongings and hurried away to Jammu. A majority of the KPs were unwilling to leave their homes. "We belong here as much as the Muslims!" declared MLA Umesh Pandita in a public rally in Srinagar moments before he was shot dead. The situation spiralled out of control, beginning with kidnappings and growing to murders. Pandits stopped stepping out of their houses but things didn't improve. That evening, incited by radicals and militant leaders, fanatics entered the towns of Sopore, Anantnag, Baramulla, Bandipora, Shopian, Awantipora, Tral, Pampore, Handwara, Kupwara, Handwara and Pulwama and painted crosses and wrote their names on houses of Pandits. Similar incidents occurred across other towns. More Pandits left the Valley in clutches, clogging the Jawahar Tunnel at Banihal as darkness descended like a bat. Kalashnikov-wielding men entered houses that had not been vacated. The occupants were thrashed within an inch of their life. Women and children were brutally raped by the militants. Men were forced to watch as their families underwent harrowing torture. The militants plundered all they could from the houses and the Pandits. They then either mowed the families down with bullets or set the houses on fire with the occupants inside, alive and breathing. The fires all over the Valley symbolised the overall scenario: Kashmir was burning. The fire was spreading and desperate measures were needed to bring it under control.

The next morning, at 10 o'clock, Lone switched on the radio and tuned into the All India Radio channel.

"It is with immense sadness and a palpable sense of fear that I bring to you confirmed news from the Press Trust. Last night, Kashmiri

Pandits fled the Valley in massive numbers. They had been receiving threats from Separatists, Radicals and militant groups for the last month or so but nobody expected the situation to spiral out of hand so drastically. The figures of refugee KPs hover somewhere around two hundred thousand. Bodies of women and children have been found in horrific states. Houses have been burnt down and it seems to be very clear that a Pandit-free Kashmir is what the Separatists, Radicals and militant groups want. The administration in New Delhi has to be held responsible for their failure in ordering the Army and other security forces to take charge of the situation. Also, in a dramatic and sudden turn of events, prominent bureaucrat Jagdeep Mahajan has been appointed the Governor of Jammu and Kashmir for a second time. Mister Mahajan arrived in Srinagar today. As a form of protest towards the appointment, the Chief Minister Doctor Farhad Ahmed has tendered his resignation, which is effective tomorrow. The people of Kashmir have shared a warm relationship with Mister Mahajan in his previous term as Governor and we hope that his appointment to the position will help in nipping the militancy problem in the bud," said the news reader.

Jagdeep Mahajan, better known as Jagdeep, had been a bureaucrat in the Indian Administrative Service before he joined the Indian Congress. He served as Lieutenant Governor of Delhi during the 1982 Asian Games. After the then Prime Minister Mrs Indu Gangasingh's assassination in 1984, he was appointed Governor of Jammu and Kashmir by her son Robin, who had succeeded her as Prime Minister. In 1989, Robin tried to convince Jagdeep to stand for Lok Sabha Elections. Jagdeep's reluctance led to a fallout with Robin and his resignation as Governor. He left the Indian Congress and joined the People's Party of India. Upon re-appointment as Governor in '90, he decided to fight fire with fire against the militants and Separatists in Kashmir. It was under his supervision that many new laws came into being in a land whose reality was alien to the rest of India.

Farhad Ahmed came from an illustrious political family. His father Sheikh Ahmed was known as the 'Lion of Kashmir'. Sheikh had possessed a charisma that his son and grandson, both Chief Ministers of Jammu and Kashmir, lacked. He had risen from humble beginnings and therefore connected with the common man. Upon Sheikh's passing, Farhad had succeeded him as the Chief Minister but was dismissed within one year by none other than Jagdeep. After the results of 1987 'notorious' Assembly Elections were declared, Farhad was accused by members from other parties of having rigged the elections in his favour with support from the Indian Congress. Syed Samiuddin, an elected member of the Assembly from Gurez constituency, was denied entry into the Assembly. He had an argument with Farhad, telling the latter that he couldn't deny an elected representative entry into the Assembly. Farhad continued with his charade. In a fit of rage, Samiuddin crossed over to Pakistan, took up arms and formed a militant group called the Hizbul Mujahideen. The Hizbul Mujahideen started to incite the people of Kashmir against Farhad and against the 'occupational forces' of India. Many young boys crossed the border and received training. They returned as heroes with that dreaded weapon, the Kalashnikov in their hands. They battled the Army in pockets and started to spread terror in the hearts of people, especially Pandits, who started to flee the Valley in small numbers.

Baig listened to the radio broadcast gravely, exchanging dark looks with Lone. Both of them were stunned to hear news of the exodus. The militants had successfully carried out the orders of their superiors. Baig rang up Colonel Pratap.

"Good Morning, sir. Baig speaking."

"Yeah, tell me."

"Sir, what is this news about the exodus?" asked Baig incredulously.

"I'm afraid it's true, Baig," Pratap's tone was low.

"But sir, how could this happen? I told you about the Hardliners' plan."

"And I immediately informed the GOC. He spoke to the Northern Army Commander, who spoke to the Chief. The Chief gave orders regarding tighter security arrangements across the Valley."

"But?!"

"Apparently, Home Minister Maqsood Shahid advised the PM to not act upon such rumours. He said that the Pandits were well-protected and never in the history of Kashmir had there been communal violence on such a large scale. And since the government in New Delhi is sitting on a chair with three legs, Sahni agreed. Last evening, we got a message from the Chief's Secretariat to disregard orders from earlier in the day."

"And look at what it has led to, sir! Blood is flowing on the streets of the Valley now! And in the eyes of the people, the Army, among others, is the culprit."

"I know, but the Army can't disregard orders from the PMO, can it?"

"That's true, sir. These bloody politicians can't do anything but bring shame to the country!"

"We'll just have to continue doing our jobs, Baig. What's done is done."

"Yes, sir."

Baig couldn't help wondering about those who were now living in fear in the Valley. The politicians had, in his mind, ruined everything. It was a certainty that Governor's Rule would now be imposed. And that is exactly what happened. Later that evening, the Motorola beeped. Lone flipped the scrambler switch on and picked up the receiver.

"Samir Ali. Give the phone to Baig," said a brisk voice.

"Baig here," said Baig as he took the phone from Lone.

"Liaquat, it's Samir. Have you heard of Jagdeep's appointment?"

"Yeah, heard it on the radio."

"Liaquat, can you hear me? What's that disturbance?"

"Must be the scrambler."

"Good god! Turn it off, Liaquat. I told you not to use one."

"Done. Can you hear me now?"

"Yeah. You?"

"All clear!"

"Okay. As his parting gift, Farhad Ahmed has imposed curfew across Srinagar. I have received some very important news so listen very carefully."

"Okay."

"Tonight, security forces will conduct door-to-door searches in the Old City area. Any suspected militant will be taken into custody with immediate effect. Be ready when the search is conducted at your hideout. We have decided not to inform the security forces of your presence so be careful."

"Right."

"And not a word to the officer conducting the search."

"Roger that!"

"Bye, Liaquat. Take care."

Liaquat kept the phone down and told Lone to follow him upstairs. Lone was filled in about the search operation and they quickly removed all traces of identification. They went up on to the terrace and from there they had a perfect view of Downtown Srinagar. Vehicles had gathered up on the wooden Gawakadal Bridge and near Burnhall School and Baig saw figures moving around in single file. A few minutes later, the people next door got the shock of their lives. Baig and Lone could make out each and every move of the CRPF men against the well-lit interiors of the house. They knocked on the door and it was opened by a young boy. 7.62 Self-Loading Rifles were pointed at him and he was told to call out to the rest of the family. Their identification was checked and then the CRPF men got inside the house to search it. They went through each of the three floors and hit jackpot on the third. Baig and Lone watched the action from across the alley. A couple of soldiers pulled and pushed at the wooden panels on the wall. One of them gave way. A tall bearded man was pulled out from behind the panelling. He was searched. Two pistols were recovered. He was thrown up against the wall and was bombarded with questions. Baig and Lone could hear the yells of the soldiers.

"Where did you get these pistols from?"

"Which group are you a part of: FLJK or Hizbul?"

"You're a militant, aren't you?"

To these queries came squealing replies.

"No, sir. They belong to a friend."

"Neither group, sir. I swear."

"I am not a militant, sir. Please believe me."

Two soldiers were sent down to call the family upstairs. The head of the family, a middle-aged chemical engineer, confessed that the man was indeed a militant. Both of them were arrested and taken away. The streets were swarming with a large number of boys and men who had been arrested. Suddenly, there was a loud knock on the front door downstairs. Baig and Lone grabbed false identity cards and rushed downstairs.

"Government servants," mumbled Lone after opening the door.

The four men paid no attention and entered the house. Baig addressed the officer.

"Officer, I am an independent contractor with the State Government."

"Everyone becomes a government servant during a crackdown. Proof of Identity?" asked the officer.

"Here," said Baig, handing the officer one of his fake ID cards.

Lone followed suit.

The officer scrutinised the two ID cards.

"Search the house," he said to his troops.

Baig and Lone were stunned.

"I work for the State Government," Baig told the officer.

"You do but in my eyes, everyone is a suspect."

"Officer, I'm sure we can make this problem go away," Lone said slimily.

"Are you trying to bribe a government servant?" the officer slapped Lone across the face.

"Please, officer. Why don't you just ask your superior whether or not we are telling the truth? Your superior is Ahlawat *sahib*, right?"

"Yes," the officer's tone had gone from obnoxious to cautious.

"Irfan, get the satellite phone for the officer," Baig commanded.

Lone was accompanied by two of the soldiers as he fetched the Motorola. He quietly handed it over to the officer. The officer dialled his superior's number. He spoke briefly before handing the phone back to Lone.

"Ahlawat *sahib* has confirmed that you are a government contractor," he said to Baig. "And also, that this loudmouth is your brother."

"I apologise for his behaviour. Can you tell me what exactly is going on here?"

"A crackdown is being carried out under orders from Chief Minister Farhad Ahmed. We have to take any suspect with us," came the reply.

"And how many have been taken so far?" interjected Lone.

"Given the happenings outside, at least a hundred. We are yet to cover a couple of areas though," said the officer. "Keep your papers nearby at all times. Crackdowns are going to become a frequent thing," finished the officer and left the compound along with his soldiers.

"What was that all about?"

"This house was previously owned by two brothers. They died a year ago in France. The Wing gave us fake IDs with their details."

"That bastard sure hit me hard!"

"You deserved it," smirked Baig.

The crackdown in Downtown Srinagar went on overnight and dawn had started to creep in by the time it ended. Just as the CRPF vehicles moved out, a call came from a nearby mosque.

"These Indian forces have taken away our loved ones. Our sons, brothers, fathers, husbands and uncles. Will we, as revolutionaries take this lying down? We will not. Rise up against these occupational forces. They have taken away our breadwinners. What is this? Is this democracy? Come out on to the streets. Don't let their machine guns frighten you. You have something that they don't. A purpose. A purpose for an Azad Kashmir. The Kashmiri Pandits are not our brothers. They're *kafirs*. They must be driven out of the Valley. If they wish to stay, they must embrace Islam. If they wish to live but not convert, kill them. Grab their women and keep them for yourselves. Mark their houses and property for yourselves. Decorate your sons and send them across the border. They will be our liberators. They will teach the Indians and the Pandits a lesson!"

Baig and Lone looked at each other and then out of the window, wondering how much time it would take for all of Srinagar to take to the streets.

**

4

MASSACRE OR SELF-DEFENCE: THE EVENING OF JANUARY 21ST 1990

Other mosques started giving out similar calls. The atmosphere had turned absolutely tense. Baig knew that Farhad Ahmed had ordered the crackdown in a fit of rage. Politicians often issued orders without thinking about the repercussions. Satellite signals had been jammed and Baig failed to get in touch with anyone from the R&AW or with Colonel Pratap. Curfew had still not been lifted and it seemed for some time as if there was not going to be a single civilian soul in Srinagar who'd dare to step out. Time passed by at a snail's pace. As far as Baig and Lone thought, Lal Chowk and the rest of Old Srinagar would be crawling with every single soldier the security forces could spare. They both sat and read through the morning. Baig was so worried that he ended up reading the same line eight times. Lone kept looking around the room every few minutes. At around twelve o'clock, Baig went up to the terrace and looked around at the area below. Everything seemed quiet. Here and there, people were peering out of their homes, as if waiting for something to happen. All of a sudden, Baig heard a loud noise. Lone came running up on to the terrace in an attempt to find the source of the noise. He scrambled up on to the roof of the house and then stood on the chimney.

"Sajid, are you out of your mind? Get back down!" snarled Baig.

"Sir, come up. You've got to see this," came Lone's voice, completely calm.

Baig jumped on to the roof like an agile cat. Lone got off the chimney so that Baig could stand on it.

"Fuck!" was all Baig could manage.

There was a huge gathering at the Ghanta Ghar in Lal Chowk. There were at least two hundred men, women and children. Some of them were holding placards, some had posters while others carried flags. They headed down Residency Road, yelling just one common slogan. A small group would yell '*Hum kya chahte?*' and the rest of the crowd would respond with '*Azadi!*' The duo stood just there, watching the crowd march on past Burnhall School. The crowd moved towards the left of National Highway 1D, better known as the Kargil-Skardu Road.

"Sir, these morons are going to go and stand either in front of Ahmed's house or in front of Papa 2!" remarked Lone.

He was wrong. The crowd went and stood in front of a palatial mansion. They were yelling themselves hoarse.

"Sajid, get the binoculars!"

Lone ran down the steps and looked through his stuff for binoculars. He pulled them out of his suitcase and hurried back to the terrace. Baig snatched them from his hands and focussed on the marching protestors.

"Sir, what is that building?" asked Lone, urgency in his voice.

"Bloody hell!" exclaimed Baig as he caught a fairly detailed view of the mansion.

Barbed wire and shards of glass sat atop the compound walls. Overseas personnel in different uniforms and with hi-tech weapons were standing at the gates, hardly perturbed by the group of people in front of them. The only striking similarity in their uniforms was the trademark sky-blue helmet of the United Nations. A large board said 'UNITED NATIONS MILITARY OBSERVER GROUP IN INDIA AND PAKISTAN'.

After Pakistan-backed tribals and subsequently, the Pakistani Army had invaded Kashmir in October 1947, the former princely state acceded to India, which sent forces into Kashmir to drive the invaders out. While the war was still on, India took the issue of Kashmir to the United Nations who, in Resolutions 39 and 47 of the Security Council, established the United Nations Commission for India and Pakistan. The UNCIP had a lot of responsibilities. The first was to see to it that Pakistan would withdraw from the territory they had captured in 1947. After this, India was supposed to withdraw the excess formations of the Indian

Army from the Valley, leaving a comparatively smaller force to maintain law and order. Following this, a plebiscite was to be held under the supervision of the UNCIP. Furthermore, the UNCIP was supposed to oversee the formation of a Ceasefire Line between India and Pakistan, which came into being after the 1949 Karachi Agreement. In 1950, the UNCIP was dissolved and the UNMOGIP was formed. Its main duty was to ensure that neither side violated the ceasefire. After the 1972 Simla Agreement and the formation of the Line of Control, India argued that the MOGIP was no longer a relevant office since its mandate was specific to the Ceasefire Line under the Karachi Agreement. The United Nations Secretary-General stated that the MOGIP could only be dissolved by a decision of the UNSC and since no such decision had been taken, the MOGIP would continue to function as it had on December 17th 1971, when ceasefire had been declared between India and Pakistan and had ended what had been the third war between the countries.

"Those fools are outside the MOGIP. Come on, Sajid. Nothing we can do here," said Baig and the two left the terrace.

As they reached the ground floor, Baig saw the Motorola's light flickering. He reached across and picked it up.

"Baig here."

"Baig, this is Colonel Pratap."

"Good Afternoon, sir."

"We are expecting a blast or some sort of militant activity in Downtown today. I want you to withdraw from the area if such a thing does happen."

"Right, sir."

Baig turned to Lone and told him to stay alert and keep necessary equipment ready.

"A blast? Today? The FLJK or the Hizbul guys would have to completely lose their heads if they are going to attempt something like that," Baig said to himself.

"Sajid, we're going to take the satellite phones and the radio upstairs. We'll bag a window seat from where we have a view of the front door. C'mon," he said after Lone had returned.

They settled themselves near a fireplace in one of the rooms on the top floor. Lone switched on the radio. It was nearly time for the AIR 4

PM broadcast. As the last notes of the folk songs died out, both men sat up and stared at the radio.

"Good Evening Srinagar. This is Rahul Mattoo of All India Radio bringing you the 4 PM broadcast. As many of you would be aware, last night, on orders of outgoing the Chief Minister Doctor Farhad Ahmed, extensive house-to-house searches were conducted across Srinagar, especially the Old City. Over six hundred men and teenage boys have been detained on suspicion of waging an internal war against the state of India. Majority of them have been charged with Section 121 of the Ranbir Penal Code. They have been taken into custody and are currently housed in different prisons across Jammu and Kashmir. Any family member who wishes to file an FIR against the detention may do so within twenty four hours of arrest and will be required to take along proof of identity of the accused family member and himself or herself. Any family member who wishes to meet with the detainee should contact the office of the Health and Family Welfare Department. The towns of Srinagar, Anantnag, Awantipora, Baramulla, Kupwara, Pulwama, Bandipora, Shopian and Sopore have been put under curfew for an indefinite period. All those who wish to leave there homes must do so in possession of proper identification and all people must indoors by 5 o'clock in the evening. Defaulters will be taken into police custody. Anyone having any information of the whereabouts of militants should please inform the police. Anyone found to be harbouring militants, in possession of illegal arms and documents, or engaging in any anti-national activity will be taken into custody and tried in court immediately. That is all from the English Desk this evening. Please tune in at 4:30 PM for the broadcast in Kashmiri by Ismail Latif. This is Rahul Mattoo from All India Radio saying goodbye."

"Well, that was short," Lone laughed.

There was a sudden gust of wind and the window panes rattled. Baig peered out. Through the gap in between houses in the lane down below, he saw a large group of protestors walking.

"Sajid, get the binoculars and follow me," he said and hurried off to the terrace.

Lone grabbed the binoculars and hurried after Baig. From the terrace, they saw around three hundred people walking towards the

Gawakadal Bridge. They were armed not with posters and banners and placards but with stones and *kangris*. The CRPF and Jammu and Kashmir Police at the bridge were on the alert. It was a tense moment. At the bridge, a man who would go down in history for all the wrong reasons took charge. Deputy Superintendent of Police Ashfaq Bashir was telling his men to be ready. The moment arrived before anyone could say "Jack Robinson". The protestors pelted the troops with the stones and *kangris*. A few troops were injured. The rest were determined. As the air was filled with coal embers and stones, DSP Bashir shouted out his orders.

"Fire!"

The 7.62 SLRs and the .303s used by the police and CRPF opened up. The troops didn't think twice before opening fire. Their action had been retaliation to the stones and embers. The helpless protestors couldn't do much. Some pretended to be dead. Some jumped into the Jhelum River which flowed under the bridge. Some tried to run for it but were hit by stray bullets. Baig and Lone watched the action unfold in a state of horror. Baig felt that the protestors shouldn't have resorted to stone- and ember-pelting but also felt that Bashir should have warned the crowd before opening fire. Blood was flowing on the wooden bridge like a river. Body parts were strewn all over the place. Bashir went around the corpses. He ascertained that the people lying there were dead. Those who flinched when he kicked them were shot immediately. The man showed absolutely no remorse.

**

5

FRICTION BETWEEN FACTIONS

Curfew was finally lifted in the week after Gawakadal. The response to this was exuberant. On January 26th, the fortieth Republic Day of India, people congregated in various public places and raised anti-India slogans. Militants fired bullets into the air. The Army and the security forces were on high alert for any activity. Movement had to be permitted since it was a public holiday. At Lal Chowk, some over-excited youths waved Pakistan's national flag while others burnt the Tricolour. Just the previous day, four Indian Air Force personnel, including a Squadron Leader, had been shot dead as they were waiting for their vehicle. On the same night, security forces searched a small town called Handwara in the district of Kupwara. Gunpowder was thrown on houses and buildings and they were burnt to the ground, leaving thousands homeless. Encounters started becoming more frequent. The locals had a common theory that all the crackdowns and encounters were part of a grand conspiracy by the Indian Army to induce fear among the people. A number of people wondered whether even a single encounter was genuine or were the bodies that were found just those of innocent under-trials and detainees who had been murdered and the incident been staged to look like an encounter. Surrendered militants signed up with the security forces and became informers. They would provide information and would earn money in return. Militant outfits became suspicious of their own numbers. The concept grew in large numbers thereafter and the informers came together to form their own secret network called the Ikhwan-e-Kashmir.

In mid-February, another meeting was called for. Baig and Lone once again went to the de-facto headquarters of the FLJK.

"Please come in, Major *sahib*," said Malik.

"Farooq *miyaan*, where is everyone else?" asked Baig.

"Nobody else has come yet. We have to be very vigilant in times like these," replied Malik.

"Did we do any demonstration in the past few days?" asked Lone.

"Yes. A lot of our young boys went to Lal Chowk and waved Pakistani flags. Our demands are simple. Why doesn't the Indian government understand?" complained Malik.

There was a knock on the door.

"*Jenab*, the others have arrived," said a teenager to Malik.

"Show them in."

Hussain entered, followed by Faisal and a middle-aged man wearing dark glasses.

"Major, how are you?" said Hussain, displaying his sparkling white teeth.

"Absolutely fine, *jenab*," replied Baig.

"*Abbu*, this is ISI Major Zulfiqar Afridi. I told you about him," said Mir Omar Faisal.

"Major *sahib*, please tell your bosses to stop trying to create the situation of a proxy war in Kashmir," said Maulana Omar Faisal sternly.

"Maulana, if the Indians keep killing our people, why should Pakistan not help us?" demanded Hussain.

"Let it be for now, *Abbu*. We can discuss this later on, Hussain *sahib*," intervened Faisal.

All six of them sat down.

"Yasir's capture was a deeply disturbing incident. He went to Sopore and the Army just got him by the scruff of his collar," said Malik.

"Why didn't you try to do anything about it, Farooq?" demanded Hussain.

"*Jenab*, the cargo of weapons is delayed due to heavy snowfall around the Muzaffarabad-Uri highway," replied Malik.

"Major, why don't you establish contact with your ISI people and get the goods from Punjab or Rajasthan?" asked Hussain.

"Hussain *sahib*, border crossings have increased so much that checks have become stringent. After Jagdeep's appointment, they have started tapping ordinary phone lines. Code words are no good either.

We will just have to make do with equipment we currently possess," explained Baig.

"Hussain *sahib*, why not try and reach out to the Indian government for a peaceful, political solution to the Kashmir issue? Why the bloodshed? More Kashmiri boys die than your targeted Indian troops!" said Maulana.

"Maulana, have you already forgotten Gawakadal? What about Manzoor Butt's hanging in Tihar six years back?" snapped Hussain.

"What about hijacking civilian aircraft? Killing Pandits? Driving them out of their properties? As for Manzoor Butt, what was the reason behind Rajiv Phadnis' murder?" countered Maulana.

"Driving the Pandits out was a necessity. They are infidels, just like Hindus all over the world. You support India, Maulana," spat Hussain.

"No, I support peace."

"What peace? Why was there never a plebiscite held? Maulana, we want freedom."

"If we had just behaved like civilised people and won over the trust of New Delhi, maybe we would have had the plebiscite. But people like you are inciting others. You are sending young boys to certain death. You are tarnishing the image of Kashmiri Muslims. Why do you think your passport was taken away?"

"You are a bloody Indian agent. I don't know why you are part of the APAKC!"

"I lead the 'Moderates', not the 'Hardliners'. Look at Yasir Meer. He followed the path of the gun and see where he has landed up. If you are so keen on promoting militancy, why don't you pick up the gun yourself? You know as well as I do that the people who have picked up the gun, or at least a majority of them, have done so in order to earn quick money. Their objective is not freedom. You want to sit comfortably in your house at Hyderpora and make anti-India comments. This is what angers them, Hussain *sahib*. If people like Farhad Ahmed and Ashfaq Bashir are responsible for Gawakadal, so are you. Your crazy remarks are creating a massive problem."

"Why are you here then? What do you attend these meetings for? To promote India?"

"I attend them out of respect for Kashmir and its people. I have never denied the fact that certain atrocities have been committed by India, never! But I'll never deny the fact that it is people like you who keep encouraging more people to cross the border. Major Afridi, your ISI people are training these boys. Please don't take this in the wrong way, but does Pakistan actually want freedom for Kashmir or does it want to rule over our land?"

"Maulana *sahib*, our nation has had a rather tragic political state of affairs. We have had constant change of power and each ruler wishes to bring something new to the table. This means that no proper decision-making mechanism has been set in place. Many elements within our country feel that the Simla Agreement was a way of paving peace for the Valley, but the Army and the ISI disagree and so does the political executive," said Baig.

"Why are you here then, Major?" Hussain turned to Baig fiercely.

"I am here to oversee the transfer of power from India to Azad Kashmir. I may be an ISI agent, but that doesn't mean I do not have a mind of my own," Baig shot back.

"Major, please relax. Hussain *sahib*, why are we bickering amongst ourselves?" said Malik.

"Maulana Omar Faisal is an Indian agent. I will call an emergency meeting of the APAKC immediately. You will be voted out, Maulana," threatened Hussain.

"Very well. Then I will inform the Indian government about all the activities going on and the controller of those activities. Hussain, do not be clouded with the misconception that you will get away scot-free if I am forced out of the APAKC. Kashmir knows only one head of the Jamia Masjid of Srinagar and his name is Maulana Omar Faisal. You cannot usurp me of that position. And as long as I am the head of the Jamia Masjid, I will make earnest attempts to put down your militant uprising," retaliated a fuming Maulana.

"You think that Kashmiri Muslims will follow you? I will declare that you are an Indian agent. You wish for Kashmir to be with India."

"Do you want Kashmir to join the political instability of Pakistan? That country too takes repressive action against its own people. Look at the people of Pakistan-occupied Kashmir. Their voices have been suppressed by the administration. And if Kashmir were to become an independent state, can you guarantee the safety of Pandits and Sikhs? What are the chances that Pakistan will not attack us and try to take Kashmir by force? I was four years old in 1947. You were nineteen. Have you forgotten what happened to women at Baramulla and Uri? Those maniacal bastards raped, murdered and looted their way to the doorstep of Srinagar. You don't mind that, Hussain. As long as your backside isn't on fire, you do not care. What political position will you occupy if we get freedom? You want to be an entire Cabinet and a President and the Chief of all Armed Forces. Your lust for power is horrifying, given that you'll do anything to get it!"

"All I wish for is freedom. Power can be distributed later on."

"You will distribute it all among Hardliners. Your sycophants will occupy all important positions. Moderates, Pandits and Sikhs will get nothing. Hussain, you will promote hatred for other communities. Kashmir will never be a peaceful place with someone like you at the helm."

"You want to be Prime Minister?" shrieked Hussain in a banshee-like voice. "A pro-Hindu man can never be a political leader in Kashmir. It is the home of a Muslim-majority population. Muslims will hold the power. I am going to call an emergency meeting of the APAKC tomorrow. We will decide your future over there, Maulana."

"Hussain, don't be under the misconception that my removal from the APAKC will deter me from political activities," Maulana wagged a finger at Hussain.

"*Jenab*, let us all go home and think over all that has been discussed. No hasty decisions. Rafiq Ibrahim will preside over the APAKC meeting tomorrow. All members will attend. Lone, Afridi, you too. We will arrange for the meeting to be held at the Nagin Lake, on one of the houseboats," said Malik.

"Who is Rafiq Ibrahim?" asked Baig.

"Rafiq Ibrahim is the leader of the Non-Aligned group of the APAKC," answered Malik.

Maulana and Faisal left first, nodding at Malik, Baig and Lone but completely ignoring Hussain.

"Bastards!" muttered Hussain as he too got up to leave.

Lone and Baig left last.

"Now you watch the fun, sir. Maulana Omar Faisal has the right ideas. Ibrahim will support him. He can't be voted out. The APAKC has to elect a new President. Hussain's term is over. The problem lies ingrained within Hussain. He is like a mental patient, the only difference being that a lot of those poor souls are nice and he isn't. He will not forget today for a long time. He will be determined to take revenge," said Lone as they drove into their compound.

A minute after they had entered the house, the FLJK satellite phone rang. Baig crossed over to the living room and picked it up.

"Farooq, we are going to murder that bastard Maulana!" came Syed Mohammed Ali Hussain's maniacal voice.

**

6

TURBULENCE: MEETING ON THE NAGIN LAKE

FEBRUARY 21ST 1990
NAGIN LAKE
SRINAGAR, INDIA

The day after the argument between Hussain and Maulana, an APAKC meeting was called for. The venue was one of the larger houseboats on the Nagin Lake, the sister of the iconic Dal. Despite the fact that curfew had been lifted, not a single soul was to be seen on the streets. The morning was bitterly cold and it had snowed a bit. As he dressed, Baig tucked his Walther P1 under his *bandhgala*. Lone too had his service revolver but he wasn't counting on it if things went wrong. According to him, six bullets weren't really going to make a difference. They set off in the 800, moving slowly since the car could skid on the sleety roads. Baig was worried. He remembered Hussain's voice and thought of how things would go downhill if Maulana was killed. He mocked the old man's foolishness at having dialled the wrong number too. They drove down Boulevard Road and parked in front of the Shankaracharya Reserve Forest. They took a *shikara* towards the Floating Market. Baig lowered his hand and the tips of fingers skimmed the freezing water.

"Sajid, what is the name of the houseboat?"

"It's called 'Imperial Regency Houseboat'."

Vendors had just started to open their stalls at the Floating Market as the *shikara* passed by. Then came the small island of Chaar Chinar, named because of the four Chinar trees that stood on it. As they

38

went around it, the lake changed drastically. In this part, there were no colourful boats. A houseboat stood some distance away. As they neared it, Baig saw four small *shikaras* bobbing up and down at each corner of the houseboat. There was one man in each *shikara*. Baig knew very well that they were actually militants posing as tradesmen, with their Kalashnikovs hidden under the rugs and grenades in the flower baskets. He thought they looked far too suspicious and told them to scatter around the houseboat. The *shikara* bobbed up and down as they jumped off. One of the men standing guard on the houseboat gave the *shikarawallah* a hundred rupee note. Once inside the houseboat, the duo was led up to the upper deck where a long table had been placed with about thirty chairs. Baig and Lone found that their seats were a few places from the head of the table. They looked out of the windows at the view outside. The Hazratbal Mosque could be seen clearly with the snow providing a scenic backdrop. Baig noticed something that looked like a combination of a mausoleum and a memorial. A CRPF bunker was next to it, along with a check point.

"Sajid, what is that?"

"That is the mausoleum of Sheikh *sahib*, the first Prime Minister of the State. CRPF personnel have been detailed to guard it because the administration is afraid of it being defaced by militants."

Baig then spotted another group of uniformed men at the banks of the Nagin. He asked one of the guards for a pair of binoculars. He squinted through them and saw a mix of CRPF and Jammu & Kashmir Police personnel standing on the banks with motor-boats. His heart took a leap.

"Sajid, there is a sizeable contingent from the security forces on the banks."

Lone too looked through the binoculars and gulped.

"Let's just hope they aren't needed today," he said.

Ten minutes later, people started arriving. First were Maulana Omar Faisal and Mir Omar Faisal.

"Afridi *sahib*, Hussain was quite upset with you yesterday," smiled Maulana.

"Indeed. In fact, I wanted to tell you something."

"I'm all ears."

"Yesterday, just after Lone and I reached the hideout, Hussain called. He had dialled the wrong number, mine instead of Farooq's. He said he wanted you killed."

"*Abbu*, this is why I told you not to come here today."

Maulana waved an impatient hand to tell his son to keep quiet.

"What?! But why are you telling this to me?"

"My job is to prevent bloodshed among Kashmiris. If the APAKC start fighting among themselves, what use will a plebiscite be?"

Just then, the Hardliners of the APAKC walked in, led by Hussain. All of them glared at Maulana, who gave them a cheery smile. They took their seats. Soon, everyone had arrived. At the head of the table sat a tall, middle-aged man who wore, unlike most others, a suit and looked well-educated. He cleared his throat and spoke.

"Good Morning, everyone. We have gathered here at the request of Syed Mohammed Ali Hussain, who heads the Hardliners of the All Party Azad Kashmir Conference. Hussain *sahib* has lodged a complaint and proposed the expulsion of Maulana Omar Faisal, leader of the Moderates. The reason cited is that Maulana *sahib* has, in a small gathering, made pro-India remarks. I, Rafiq Ibrahim, leader of the Non-Aligned, have been appointed Chairman of this meeting. We will listen to both arguments and reach a decision. The panel will consist of Abbas Shah, who recently joined us in an administrative role; Hamid Qureshi and me. The second matter at hand is the election of the new APAKC President, since Hussain *sahib's* term is finishing at the end of this month. The new President will take charge on March 1st 1990. Hussain *sahib*, you may begin."

Hussain stood up. A cunning smile spread across his bearded face.

"On February 20th, five of us met at the headquarters of the Front for Liberation of Jammu and Kashmir. With me were Farooq Malik, Major Zulfiqar Afridi of the ISI, Sajid Lone, Mir Omar Faisal and Maulana Omar Faisal. Over there, an argument between Maulana and me started. He accused me of sending hundreds of young boys across the border for training like goats for slaughter. He stated that I have ulterior motives when it comes to our demands. It is for the freedom of Kashmir from occupational Indian forces that we're doing this. We have taken up arms for a cause. A cause that Maulana clearly doesn't seem to believe in. Our people have been picked up from their homes and have disappeared. Should we do nothing about this? Maulana says that we should try and hold talks with the Indian government. Why should we do such a thing? Moreover, Maulana accused me of being power-hungry. I simply stated that if Kashmir does become independent, a pro-India and a pro-Hindu person cannot possibly be in a position of power. The population of Kashmir is a Muslim-majority. What will they think if Hindus and their supporters wield power? That's all I have to say."

Maulana Omar Faisal stood up. He didn't look surprised by Hussain's argument.

"Thank you for saying what you did, Hussain. I now know more than enough to contradict your feeble argument. Gentlemen, are we not provoking the security forces into taking action against us by sending people across the border to Pakistan? They come back and wilfully fire upon anyone in uniform. The forces react as any human would. We provoke these attacks. Women are widowed when their husbands are killed. The crackdowns by the Army are based on grounds of suspicion. If militants are forcing themselves into the houses of innocent people and the latter are arrested, then no one has the right to blame the Army for picking them up. If the issue is resolved peacefully, then people will not die, they will not 'disappear'. I urge the Conference to think this through. Are we really fighting for the freedom of Kashmir or are we helping Pakistan gain control? If Hussain holds Kashmir so valuable and so close to his heart, he will agree with the fact that we need to confer with both Indian and Pakistani governments to bring an end to this issue."

Silence reigned for a few minutes.

"We have now heard both sides of the argument. Abbas *sahib*, Hamid *sahib*, if you will please follow me to the next room, we'll confer about our decision over there," said Ibrahim.

Shah and Qureshi followed him to an adjoining room. The rest of the people at the congregation started gossiping about the new wife of so-and-so and that new beautiful Indian actress and how unfortunate it was that her nationality was against her. Fifteen minutes later, Ibrahim, Shah and Qureshi re-entered the room.

"We have reached a conclusion regarding Syed Mohammed Ali Hussain's complaint against Maulana Omar Faisal. The vote has fallen three-nil in the favour of Maulana. Hussain *sahib*, we request you not to bring forth a matter which is personal in nature again. Regarding the change in leadership, you will all have noticed that you have slips kept in front of you. The Hardliners and the Moderates will both field one candidate each. The Non-Aligned have decided not to field a candidate for this term. You can tick either the box in front of APAKC-H or the one in front of APAKC-M. Hardliners, who is your candidate? Moderates?" announced Ibrahim.

"Hussain *sahib* will re-enter the fray," said a puny Hardliner.

"We put forth the name of Maulana Omar Faisal," said Mir Omar Faisal in a low voice.

"You have two minutes, gentlemen. The candidates cannot vote," said Ibrahim and looked at his pocket-watch.

Everyone started taking out pens and ticking the box of their choice. Baig and Lone exchanged a brief look before ticking APAKC-H. Two minutes later, Ibrahim called a halt and the ballots were all collected and handed over to him. He took out a large book and with some help from Shah and Qureshi, made tally marks. He removed the sheet he had been writing on and wrote with an ink pen in a blank space in the book.

"Congratulations, Maulana *sahib*. You win by seventeen votes to eleven in Hussain *sahib's* favour. You will assume office as President of the All Party Azad Kashmir Conference on the 1st of March 1990. Please name your nominee to preside over meetings in case you are unable to attend or who will assume presidency in case of your tenure ending prematurely," said Ibrahim.

"I nominate my son and deputy chairman of the Moderates, Mir Omar Faisal, as my replacement in case there is any requirement for one," said Maulana.

"Thank you, everyone. That will be all for now. The next meeting date will be fixed at Maulana *sahib's* discretion. Let us remember to stay cautious in these times and not to provoke anything that can harm the common Kashmiri," said Ibrahim gravely.

Everyone stood up and started fiddling around with their clothes, straightening them out. Suddenly, there was a burst of weapon fire. Everyone dropped to the floor. Baig crawled towards the door and looked down on to the deck. An over-enthusiastic youth had opened fire in the direction of the banks where the security forces were standing. The CRPF men leapt into the boats and started off towards the houseboats, their weapons blazing out retaliatory fire. The police personnel opened fire on the houseboat from their position on the banks of the lake. A stray bullet struck Farooq Malik on the head as he made a run for it and blood shot out like water from a hosepipe. A couple of seconds later, Malik's brain spilled out along with a lot of funny looking things. Just as Hussain was attempting to jump into one of the *shikaras*, a bullet struck him in the butt. He wailed in pain. Baig and Lone didn't fancy spending a cold night in a police lock-up. The militants in the *shikaras* also opened fire on the CRPF boats. One of the CRPF men fired a rocket. It missed its mark terribly, hitting the water instead and creating a massive fountain. Baig beckoned Lone over to the spot where he was crouching. Without turning anywhere and using the new fountain as cover, they leaped into the freezing lake. The water inside looked all green and creepy, rather unlike its pleasant blue surface. Baig felt numb but with bullets entering the water, he decided to get going. He signalled Lone to follow him and both of them navigated through the weed-filled water with agility. After spending a lung-exhausting three minutes under water, both men pulled their heads out. They had come a good thirty metres from the houseboat, where CRPF men had placed all the FLJK militants, Hussain and his buddies under arrest. They were being led away via boat and the others stood on the deck, talking to a police team. Baig and Lone swam a little more and then leapt on to a *shikara* and told the *shikarawallah* to take them to the main entrance of the lake. They rushed back to their 800, ignoring the looks they were being given by shopkeepers and raced back to Downtown. Shivering in the cold, both went for hot baths and changed into warm clothing. As soon as they'd finished getting ready, they raced down to the drawing room.

"I suppose I should give the Wing a call," said Baig and reached out for the Motorola.

Just as he picked it up, it rang. Puzzled, he pressed the green button.

"This is Colonel Pratap."

"Good Morning, sir."

"Baig, weren't you and Lone at the meeting a while back?"

"We were, sir."

"Tell me what happened."

Baig narrated the happenings of the meeting.

"The fire originated from the houseboat?" asked the Colonel.

"Yes, sir. One of the more enthusiastic militants opened fire."

"Okay. Now, this is what happened after you two decided to emulate Mark Spitz. I'll keep it brief since I have a conference to attend. Farooq Malik took a bullet to the head and died on the spot. Hussain and all other Hardliners have been taken into custody. Maulana Omar Faisal, Rafiq Ibrahim, Mir Omar Faisal and all of their mates are currently being questioned at Crime Branch by senior police officers and local Intelligence Bureau officers. I don't think charges will be pressed against them. That's all I know. Keep in touch, Baig!"

"Right, sir."

Baig dialled the number of Samir Ali next.

"Liaquat. Are you and Lone fine?"

"Yeah, don't worry."

"What the heck do you mean by 'don't worry'? Your sister has given me three calls since the incident was reported by those AIR buggers. She is convinced that you're dead. Give her a ring after you're done talking to me."

"Wait! How the hell does Shehnaaz know?" Baig demanded indignantly.

"Never mind that! What made Masarat Khan open fire?" Ali hurriedly changed the subject.

"I suspect he got a bit carried away when he saw so many uniforms standing in one place. He didn't take a single bullet is what I know. What happened after we left?"

"A CRPF sharpshooter took a clean shot at Masarat when he was reloading. Shot through the heart. He was sixteen."

There was silence at Baig's end. Masarat Khan's age and actions took him back a few years. According to official records, his father, Khaleel Baig, a Junior Commissioned Officer in the Army, had two sons and a daughter with his wife Hafiza. Shehnaaz and Mudassar were twins, born in 1955 and Liaquat came next in 1959. The record didn't state the names of Khurram and Pervez. The twins were found by Mudassar and Liaquat when they were playing cricket near a stream. They were newborns who had been abandoned by their parents. They were brought up by Khaleel and Hafiza as if they were the couple's own children. At the age of thirteen, they disappeared. Everyone thought that they'd either been kidnapped or had fallen into the stream while playing football when in fact, they had been coerced into joining the FLJK and had crossed the LC from Uri sector into Muzaffarabad. They had trained for a year and a half over there before coming back home. At the time, their father was deployed at Siachen Glacier. Mudassar was in Bihar, fighting Naxals. Liaquat was with his unit in Nagaland and Shehnaaz was in Bombay, completing her Master's degree. The twins started participating in extortion cases and the murders of prominent pro-India locals. Angered as he was by the situation, Liaquat was unable to do anything. The boys, along with their buddies, moved from place to place, avoiding detection. When Subedar Baig got this piece of news, he erupted like a volcano but, much like Liaquat, couldn't do anything about the situation. His battalion moved out of Siachen to Anantnag. One day, they got a piece of information about a group of terrorists hiding in a village nearby. A squad was selected. Subedar Baig was the senior-most JCO of the party. They set off in their vehicles, halting every few minutes to form squads on the roads and in the lanes. Teams went into houses to search them. As Subedar Baig's team moved to the centre of the village, AK-47s opened up from inside a house. As he directed men to cordon off the house and provide covering fire, the Subedar and two NCOs ran into the house. As soon as the front door was broken down, the three men quickly silenced one terrorist. Unknown to them, the ceiling was a false plywood one. In an upstairs room, the remaining four terrorists got ready for the next stage of their plan. They fired a short burst on the plywood and injured one NCO. Subedar Baig directed the other NCO to move the injured man to one of the rooms on the upper floor. They heard footsteps. They went up to the first floor cautiously and searched for the militants. They found no one. The injured man was taken to a small room which was filled with cupboards. He was helped on to an armchair. Subedar Baig noticed the cupboards. He ran across the room and opened them and started throwing clothes out. The other NCO helped him. The experienced Subedar had an inkling that one of the cupboards would have a false back. His hopes were dashed when none of the backs gave way. As a last ditch effort, he decided to open the smaller built-in cupboards on top of the ones that had just been stripped of their contents. He opened the first one and hit out at the back with the butt of his rifle. In doing that, he lost his balance. That was just as well because as soon as the back gave way, a burst of fire came through from the other end. Subedar Baig got up from the floor. He had been taken aback, by the fall and the burst. He quickly regained his composure and cautiously pulled himself back on top of the cupboard he had fallen off. He wiped his brow. He reloaded his rifle and fixed the bayonet. He motioned to the other two to load their rifles and fire at the ceiling. Splinters and large pieces of wood came flying down but there was no response. Subedar Baig waited for them to empty the magazines and then signalled them to wait. He crawled up through the hole in the wall. He crouched on the landing and saw four figures. The two taller men were preparing Molotov Cocktails. The other two figures had pinned down the cordon with suppressing fire through small vents. He could make out that the two making the Cocktails were experienced men whereas the other two were a part of the 'neither-here-nor-there' category. In a flash, he shot the tall men dead and injured their mates. He disarmed them but couldn't make out their faces due to the darkness. He turned the lights on and was stunned when he saw his two youngest children crouching before him. In a fit of rage, he opened fire yet again, killing them. Subedar Baig was broken. He was awarded the Ashoka Chakra by the President on the Independence Day 1985. The incident took a lot out of a man who had always taught his children to tread the correct path, never hesitating to punish them if they did wrong. He retired from the Army at the relatively young age of fifty, despite the fact that he was about to be promoted to Subedar Major. No one questioned his actions or ever mentioned Khurram and Pervez again. Nobody but the Baig family, Khaleel's colleagues and friends in the Army and the neighbours knew of their existence. Liaquat was informed of this over the phone. He was devastated to hear that his brothers were no more but was immensely proud that his father had put national security ahead of his family.

"Liaquat, can you hear me?" asked Ali.

"Yes. I was just remembering something that happened a long time back. What's the new plan?"

"I have come across some information. Major Zulfiqar Afridi has been ordered to attend a major meeting in Muzaffarabad. Thapar and I have come up with an idea. Of eliminating ISI chief Lieutenant General Mushtaq Niazi and Pakistan Army Chief General Hilal Bakhshi."

"When is this meeting?"

"In a month's time. On the 23rd of March. That's Pakistan Day."

"Alright. I want a team of three men each from the NSG and the MARCOS and one officer, either a Lieutenant or a Captain, from one of the battalions in Uri. Eight of us. We'll cross the border from Uri sector. Colonel Pratap will inform the concerned battalion. Just arrange the squad. I will lead the operation. Sajid can be given the day off!"

"I'll see what I can do."

"I'll call you tomorrow regarding any weapons and explosives we may require."

Baig put down the Motorola. He told Lone to switch on the radio. Lone brought the set down to the drawing room and switched to the All India Radio frequency.

"Good Afternoon. I am Rahul Mattoo and it's time for the one o'clock news. Our first bulletin. The APAKC held a meeting on a houseboat at the Nagin Lake today. We were informed that just as the meeting ended, one of the guards opened fire on security forces at the banks of the Lake. The forces responded in kind. The incident resulted in two deaths for the APAKC. The gunman who fired the first rounds and wanted militant leader Farooq Malik were killed. Two men, one of whom is a suspected ISI agent, jumped off the boat during a lull in the firing. The ISI agent is known as Major Zulfiqar Afridi and the Crime Branch of the Jammu and Kashmir Police has launched a search operation to capture this man before he can flee across the International Border."

Baig remembered that he had to call his sister. He dialled the extension code on the Motorola. The Army Telephone Exchange in Srinagar patched him on to a secure civilian network. He dialled one of the few telephone numbers he had ever memorised.

"Liaquat, is that you?" asked a voice at the other end.

Baig recognised it as his brother-in-law Randeep's.

"Randeep *bhai*, it is me. How are you? When did you get back from New York?"

"I'm fine. Just got back this morning."

"You must be exhausted."

"Jet lag is a cruel thing, Liaquat."

"Then let me not keep you occupied any longer, else your wife will tick me off for blabbing. Is she around?"

"Yes, I'll just call her. Bye."

"Bye."

The receiver was kept down and Randeep called out loudly. Baig heard hurried footsteps and braced himself.

"Liaquat, why in the name of God did you not give me a ring?" yelled Shehnaaz.

"Pipe down, you mad woman! Despite the hi-tech satellite phone that I have, it does not function underwater. I am perfectly fine. And how did you know that I may have been involved in the incident?"

"Remember the day you dropped by after your meeting with your boss? After you left, I gave Samir a ring and he gave me a gist of what your job would be,"

"That ass," muttered Baig.

"Don't you go after him now. I forced him to tell me. And I have a right to know. After Mudassar, Pervez and Khurram, you are my only sibling. Do I have to ask permission to know about your well being?"

"No," replied Baig quietly.

He hated being shouted at by his sister.

"Good. I want you to give me periodic phone calls. Once a week would be perfectly fine. Anyway, I have to leave for the university now. Bye!"

"Wait! Did you tell that clown anything?"

"No, I didn't. Now, if you don't mind, I'm off."

Baig heard the click of the receiver and kept the Motorola down. He called out to Lone and told him that he was going for a walk. He set out on the cold, empty lanes and streets, passing by the UNMOGIP and the Badami Bagh Cantonment. This was not the way the operation was to be going. He had to earn back the trust of the Hardliners. A van of the CRPF passed by. Baig caught the glimpse of a handcuffed man being taken away. That's when he hit upon a brilliant idea.

**

7

A PLAN

Baig hurried back to the hideout. He told Lone about his idea. Lone rubbed his hands in glee.

"I'll make the call, sir," he said.

He picked up the Motorola and dialled the police hotline.

"Police hotline? I am Inspector Sajid Wali Lone and I wish to speak to the officer in charge at the Crime Branch."

A moment later, a soft voice spoke, "DSP Vijay Khanna, Crime Branch."

"Good Afternoon, sir. Sajid here."

"Lone, what a pleasant surprise. How are you?"

"Fine, sir. Can you do me a favour?"

"Yeah, tell me."

"If you remember, the R&AW recruited me some months back for a special assignment. I need to speak to Syed Mohammed Ali Hussain, who, if my information is correct, is currently being held at Crime Branch."

"Okay. Hold on for a minute."

A minute later, the receiver was picked up and Hussain spoke.

"Sajid *miyaan*, what happened?"

"Hussain *sahib*, Major Afridi wishes to speak to you."

Baig took the Motorola from Lone.

"*Assalaam Waleiqum*, Hussain *sahib*."

"*Waleiqum Assalaam*. Sajid said you wanted to speak to me about something?"

"Yes. Have you any idea whether you will be further detained?"

"I will be. They are shifting me to Papa 2 tomorrow morning. That bastard of a Maulana must have squealed during interrogation. I want both you and Lone to stay indoors. They will raid the Lal Chowk hideout and my home in Hyderpora. If they come across any document concerning you, it will be difficult to escape."

"Don't worry, Hussain *sahib*. Lone and I are going to break you out of police custody. I will relay information to the FLJK to guard the hideouts."

"But I am being accorded top-notch security during the transfer to Papa 2," Hussain was unable to keep the pride out of his voice. "How will you be able to defeat the police?"

"We'll try something out of the book. You are the most popular leader in all of Kashmir. You are vital to everything my country and organisation stand for when it comes to Kashmir."

"*Inshallah,* you will succeed. I am disconnecting now. *Khuda Hafiz!*"

Baig heard the click of the receiver. He turned both satellite sets off.

"Sir, why are you turning the sets off?" asked Lone.

"Listen to my plan," said Baig.

Over the next five minutes, they chalked out a plan of how to get Hussain out of police custody. Then, Baig switched the satellite phones back on. He used the Motorola to dial the number of Colonel Pratap.

"Good Afternoon, sir. Baig here."

"Baig, hi. What's up?"

"Sir, I have an idea of how to get Hussain out. We can't let him live a comfortable life behind bars on minor charges. Spoils the very purpose of our work."

"I agree. What's your plan?"

"Tomorrow morning, Hussain is being transferred from Crime Branch to Papa 2. If we were to hijack the convoy and get him out, he'd be over the moon."

"That's true. But you'll need to pull off something that can't be replicated on the silver screen. The firing has to be real. And I don't think you need to be told that you can't kill policemen."

"I have given that factor a lot of thought. What if we could procure Kevlar vests for the policemen?"

"Kevlar could do the trick. But the cargo will have to come from Manesar if we are to consider that possibility."

"I have some useful contacts that could help us out. Over the Kevlar could be a standard-issue vest, in which we can pack red, blood-like liquid. We fire at the convoy, supposedly wound and kill some policemen, get Hussain and leave the area immediately. We'll use old SLRs and pistols, if that can be arranged."

"I'll arrange for some to be borrowed from the CRPF. What else?"

"Sir, I need the PRO of the Corps HQ to tell the media that two patrolling CRPF men were taken down by two FLJK chaps. This should reach AIR latest by eight o'clock this evening so that it will be announced during 8:30 bulletin tomorrow morning. That's all, sir. And I would like it if you could brief DSP Vijay Khanna of Crime Branch about this."

"Where do you plan to have the vests dropped off?"

"I'll ask for twenty vests to be sent via chopper to Shariefabad Garrison or to the JAKLI Regimental Centre in Old Airport Military Station."

"Okay. I'll give you an update as soon as possible."

"Right, sir."

Baig dialled Nikhil Thapar's office next.

"Nikhil here."

"Hi, sir! Liaquat here."

"How are you and Sajid holding up? Everything okay?"

"We're in the pink of health. Since Hussain is now in police custody, I have devised a neat little plan to get him out."

Baig launched into the story and the plan and the requirements and Thapar listened quietly without interrupting.

"Sir, have you heard of a Colonel Sanjay Jadhav?"

"Yeah. Vaguely. He's with the NSG at the moment."

"I know. He was the Commanding Officer of the SAG I was posted in. I need you to ask a favour from him."

"Yeah. Tell me."

"I need you to ask him to provide twenty Kevlar vests. Then, I want you to get the ADG of Army Aviation to sanction one helicopter which will transport the vests to Shariefabad Garrison."

"That's a lot of work, Liaquat."

"I know, sir. But it is essential that all of this is sanctioned within three hours."

"I'll get on it right away," said Thapar.

Lone and Baig fine-tuned the plan over the next hour and a half until the Motorola beeped again.

"Liaquat, Nikhil here."

"Yes, sir?"

"I've spoken to Colonel Jadhav. He said that he can arrange for the vests. Major General Irani, the ADG of Army Aviation, agrees with the urgency of the matter but has to get the sanction from the Chief of Army Staff."

"Sir, why don't you directly speak to the Chief, General Ved Singhania?"

"I'm not too sure about speaking to General Singhania. The two of us don't get along."

"Sir, try once at least. Please."

"I'll see what I can do."

"Thank you, sir."

An hour passed. Baig started getting jittery. Air traffic in Srinagar was restricted to one chopper every half-hour after seven. At a quarter past four, the Motorola beeped.

"Baig here."

"Liaquat, Nikhil speaking."

"Yes, sir?"

"I've spoken to General Singhania. He has given the green light for our chopper demand."

"That's great. The old man's a real sport!"

"I have spoken to Vijay Khanna of Crime Branch. Colonel Pratap had told me that he may need to be convinced. He has said that he'd like to speak to you as soon as possible. The chopper will take off from Race Course Camp in ten minutes. It will land at Shariefabad Garrison at ten minutes past six. The vests will be taken to Zadibal Police Station. You should be at Shariefabad to do a check of the vests. If there is any problem, call Colonel Jadhav. He'll call the chopper back and help you out."

"Got it, sir."

"All the best, Liaquat. Get this done."

"Right, sir."

Baig disconnected the call and gave Lone a shout. He strolled in, puffing away on a cigarette. He hurriedly stubbed it when Baig gave him a glare.

"Give Khanna a ring."

"On it, sir."

Lone dialled Khanna's office on the Motorola and hurriedly spoke a few words before handing the device to Baig.

"Major Liaquat Baig, Research & Analysis Wing."

"DSP Vijay Khanna, Crime Branch."

"I assume that Nikhil Thapar has spoken to you, Mister Khanna. Am I right?"

"Yes, Mister Baig."

"Major Baig, DSP *sahib*, not Mister," Baig's tone was sharp and cold.

"Sorry, Major Baig. What's the plan then?

"Sajid and I will go to Shariefabad this evening. Once I have checked the Kevlar vests, they'll be dispatched to Zadibal Police Station. You will move Hussain at exactly 0730 hours from your location. Sajid and I will wait for you near Burnhall School. We'll stop the movement at Gupkar Road. You will be in a white Maruti Gypsy in front with two men; behind you will be a van in which there will be seven policemen and Hussain in handcuffs. Hussain's face should be covered with a black hood, the kind used in hangings. Are your men good actors?"

"They aren't NSD quality, but they'll be proficient enough."

"Good. Also, I want the police spokesperson to hype the thing up a bit, so that the escapade seems more daring. I want the report to say that we killed eight of the ten-man squad."

"I'm sure that can be arranged."

"Thank you, Mister Khanna. You've been of great help."

**

8

THE ESCAPADE

FEBRUARY 22ND 1990
CRIME BRANCH HQ
SRINAGAR, INDIA

Rain pelted down across Srinagar. The weather was bitterly cold. At Crime Branch, DSP Vijay Khanna and his team were all set. All of them wore Kevlar vests under three layers of clothing and a regular bullet-proof vest. They readied their weapons. At 7:30, Syed Mohammed Ali Hussain, attired in a white kurta-pyjama and handcuffs, was brought outside. He was shivering. Thanks to the ISI and the Government of Pakistan, he'd always lived in comfort. He was shoved into the back of a van with a black hood over his head. He felt as if he was being taken to the gallows. Even the thought of being rescued in a while didn't comfort him. Once the convoy was ready, Khanna phoned Lone.

"We're leaving."

He got into his white Maruti Gypsy and set off. They moved slowly since they couldn't afford the vehicles slipping or sliding. Khanna was extremely nervous, unlike his supremely confident namesake from a blockbuster film seventeen years ago.

*

In their hideout, Baig and Lone cleared away all of their official paraphernalia. The Motorola, documents and IDs were all put into sealed waterproof bags and dropped it into the water tank on the roof. They were wearing CRPF uniforms. They slung the ancient SLRs over their shoulders and holstered two country-made revolvers. As soon as they got Khanna's call, they locked the house and got into the 800, Baig taking the wheel. The rain was still coming down hard. They set off at a decent speed. The car wasn't stopped by anyone. They stopped at the gates of Burnhall School.

"Keep your eyes peeled, Sajid," said Baig.

A few minutes later, the two police vehicles passed the UNMOGIP and turned onto Gupkar Road. Baig stepped on the accelerator and set off in pursuit. The convoy was very slow and suddenly halted opposite the Shankaracharya Reserve Forest. From a distance, Baig and Lone saw two gun-toting masked men. In the Gypsy, Khanna was taken aback. Baig ordered Lone to open up. Lone pulled himself out of the window and on to the roof of the car. He aimed and fired two perfect headshots. The 800 skidded to a stop in front of the Gypsy and Baig and Lone got out. A policeman ran towards them. Baig and Lone fired at him. He fell, blood-like liquid spurting out of his chest. Lone knocked out Khanna and his driver and then destroyed their wireless set. Then, along with Baig, he rained bullets on the other vehicle, supposedly killing two more personnel. Hussain's captors jumped out and opened fire on the duo. Baig and Lone kept up the staged firefight until all the policemen were lying on the road. Baig jumped into the van, smashed Hussain's handcuffs and then removed the hood.

"Wow, Major. Thank you."

"Let's go."

Hussain and Baig jumped out of the van. Lone blew off the van's tyres. Baig and Lone picked up Khanna and his driver and chucked them into the van. They picked up the 'dead' policemen and threw them in as well. Lone got into the Gypsy and drove off. Baig and Hussain sat in the 800 and followed Lone. As they passed the van, Baig surveyed the scene. The van had so many bullet holes that any passer-by would think that something had actually happened there. They saw CRPF personnel running towards the van. Lone returned their salute and shouted out random orders which were quickly obeyed. He went off towards Lambert Lane while Baig and Hussain returned to the hideout. In Lambert Lane, no shop had opened yet. Lone left the Gypsy at a corner and entered a public toilet. He stripped off the CRPF uniform, under which he was wearing a tracksuit, and took an auto-rickshaw back to Maisuma-Gawakadal. When he entered the hideout, Baig and Hussain were sitting in the drawing room with the radio on.

"Good Morning. My name is Rahul Mattoo and it's time for the AIR News at 8:30. Last evening, two patrolling CRPF personnel were killed in cold blood in Maisuma-Gawakadal by men who are suspected to be a part of the FLJK's Azad Kashmir Fauj. When the bodies were discovered half an hour back, the uniforms and weapons were missing. This morning, when a team from the Crime Branch was moving Syed Mohammed Ali Hussain, leader of the APAKC Hardliners, to prison, they were accosted by two militants of an unknown terror group on Gupkar Road. The gunmen were shot dead by members of the FLJK's militant wing, the AKF, before they could do any damage. The AKF militants succeeded in killing eight policemen and injuring two, including the Crime Branch chief DSP Vijay Khanna. These men were in CRPF uniform, which leads investigators to believe that they may have planned and executed last evening's killings. They aided Hussain and escaped from the scene in DSP Khanna's white Maruti Gypsy. The vehicle has not been found yet but it is possible that it may have been abandoned. The police believe that Hussain and the two militants may be holed up in Downtown Srinagar. This escapade comes a day after Hussain and other APAKC Hardliners were detained by the Crime Branch after security forces personnel were fired upon from their meeting place in Nagin Lake. Meanwhile, newly appointed President of the APAKC, Maulana Omar Faisal, has condemned the incident and has said that the FLJK should have explored legal options in order to get Hussain acquitted but have gone and made matters worse. Yesterday, in a rare occurrence for the Budget Session, the Lok Sabha opposition, led by ex-PM Robin Gangasingh, demanded the removal of Jagdeep Mahajan as Governor of Jammu and Kashmir and demanded that fresh elections be called for in the state immediately."

Hussain sat back. Baig and Lone looked at him. All of a sudden, he started cackling.

"Those Indian bastards are running scared now. Elections! A kick from me on their asses is a more likely conclusion. And Maulana, the peace- and India-loving dimwit is not going to be able to do much. Anyway, what has happened after my arrest?"

"The Army is monitoring all known FLJK hideouts and your house in Hyderpora. Farooq was killed in the CRPF assault yesterday. Maulana, Ibrahim and the rest are also being watched," replied Baig.

"Farooq's death will be a hard hit for the AKF. He was a favourite among the boys. They've lost both of their commanders. I was hoping to choose Yasir Meer's successor soon but I don't think we can delay it any longer. Sajid *miyaan*, you handle his battalion. Major, you can take over Farooq's battalion and overall command of the AKF," Hussain announced rather pompously.

"As one of my first directives, I'd like to suggest that you leave Srinagar for the time being. We can move you immediately but you need to pick the location," Baig sounded equally pompous.

"I pick Lahore," Hussain's reply was instantaneous.

"We'll drop you off at the airport but we need you to be disguised," said Lone.

"One of my passports has me sporting a French beard. According to that passport, I'm a professor of economics at Delhi University."

"Great. Lone, go to Residency Road and pick out some ordinary clothes for Hussain *sahib*. I'll alert the ISI," said Baig.

Lone went off to Residency Road and Hussain went to the bathroom to trim and dye his beard and hair. Baig grabbed the sub-standard FLJK satellite phone. He dialled one of the numbers that he had found in Zulfiqar Afridi's documents.

"*Assalaam Waleiqum*. Major Zulfiqar Afridi speaking."

"*Waleiqum Assalaam*, Afridi. Colonel Haroon Gilani here."

"Sir, you may be aware of the fact that Syed Mohammed Ali Hussain was arrested yesterday. I have managed to get him out of police custody but I feel he should leave India immediately."

"That bloody fool! I had specifically told him to avoid meeting in public places. Fly him to Delhi. From there, tell him to board a plane for Ahmedabad. From there, he should move by road to Jamnagar. I'll send a boat and two men for him."

"Right, sir."

"I hope you haven't forgotten our meeting on Pakistan Day."

"I'll be there, sir."

"Alright. All the Best! And Afridi, try to get better soon."

"Sir?"

"Your cough. Your voice is sounding extremely hoarse."

"Oh, that. Yes, sir. I'll try and get better. I deeply appreciate your concern, sir. Thank you."

"*Khuda Hafiz*, Afridi."

"*Khuda Hafiz*, sir."

**

9

THE MUZAFFARABAD MASTERSTROKE

MARCH 23RD 1990
PAKISTAN

The cavalcade of vehicles sped out of General Headquarters, Rawalpindi. The Pakistani Rangers led the way in two jeeps. Following them were Colonel Shahriyar Haq and Colonel Haroon Gilani in a black Mitsubishi Pajero. Behind them, in a Honda Accord with the Pakistan Army flag fluttering on the bonnet and four stars on the number plate was General Hilal Bakhshi, the Pakistan Army Chief; followed by the Chief of the Inter-Services Intelligence, Lieutenant General Mushtaq Niazi, in a Honda City and three more jeeps filled with Rangers. The journey to Muzaffarabad took over four hours. The cavalcade zoomed past the picturesque hills of Murree, the rain slowing them down considerably. It was still snowing on the tall mountains nearby. At 12:30, the vehicles reached Camp 9 in Muzaffarabad. They were met by an over-enthusiastic young Captain. A Major stood close by, watching the scene like a hawk.

"Hi!" said Bakhshi jovially, walking over to him.

"Major Zulfiqar Afridi reporting for duty, sir," the officer snapped to attention.

*

MARCH 22ND 1990
FLJK HIDEOUT, MAISUMA-GAWAKADAL
SRINAGAR, INDIA

Baig paced up and down the living room. He had a lot on his mind. Thapar was to give him a call any minute. He was alone at the place he now called home. Lone had been given the day off. He had gone home to spend some time with his family. Baig would be gone by the time he got back. Baig looked at his watch just as it struck half-past eleven. The Motorola beeped. He leapt over the sofa, punched the green button and put the phone to his ear.

"Liaquat, Nikhil here."

"Good Morning, sir."

"All set?"

"Raring to go, sir."

"Good. Now, without interrupting, let me explain the plan to you. As per your instructions to Samir, three NSG commandos and three MARCOs have been chosen plucked for this assignment, though I wish the thought of using men from the SFF had occurred to me earlier. The officer designated to be the team's 2IC will meet up with you in Uri. The commandos have been briefed about the operation and have been supplied with assault rifles, sniper rifles, a Glock 17 with silencer and extra ammo, grenades and one RPG launcher. Also, you'd told Samir you wanted a PMN-1 Anti-Personnel Mine. You'll find two of those. The operation has been given limited sanction by the Prime Minister's Office. In the event that you get caught or killed, the government will exercise..."

"Plausible deniability!" interrupted Baig.

"Did you not hear me forbid you from interrupting? In case of such a scenario, your pension will be passed on to your oldest surviving family member, your father."

"Yes. I'm familiar with the entire procedure," Baig sounded bored.

"Colonel Pratap has already sent a team to pick you up. You'll be 'arrested'. Take what you need, disable the satellite phones and tell those guys to lock the house. All the best, Liaquat!"

"Thank you, sir. *Jai Hind!*"

He removed the batteries from both satellite phones and hid all official documents. He left Lone a coded note explaining where everything was hidden. All of his work having been completed, Baig waited patiently for the arrival of the 'Arrest Party'. They arrived soon. Baig was handcuffed and marched out. He instructed one of the men to lock the house. He was pushed into a jeep and the party set off. As soon as the jeep entered the gates of Badami Bagh, one of the men opened Baig's handcuffs. The jeep stopped outside the main building of the Corps Headquarters. Baig got off and followed a runner to Colonel Pratap's office. He entered the room. Sitting behind a spotless desk was an officer in his forties, playing with a paperweight.

"*Jai Hind*, sir!" said Baig.

"Hi, Baig. Sit down. I received a message from the R&AW chief this morning. He gave me a brief idea of the situation. Your team is waiting for you at the firing range. I have also alerted a couple of battalions along the LC. Your main contact will be a unit of the Maratha Light Infantry. A Lieutenant of theirs, Neil Kapoor, is the other officer on your team. He will brief you about the situation at the LC. Try and cross back by midnight tomorrow. Be careful. Muzaffarabad is a massive garrison. They get a single hint of the presence of a spy and that'll be it! Your team is waiting for you at the firing range. Good luck!"

"Thank you, sir!"

Baig took a lift in a passing Shaktimaan to the firing range. Over there, he saw six men gathered around a table. He walked up to them.

"So, you're the men. *Jai Hind*!"

"*Jai Hind*, sir!" they chorused.

"I recognise Ranjit, Khalid and Sunil from the NSG. You three must be the MARCOS?" Baig enquired of the others.

"Yes, sir. I'm Petty Officer Vineet Tripathi and these two are Leading Seaman Rakesh Chand and Seaman 1 Thomas Srinivasan," replied the senior-most MARCO.

"Good. I am Major Liaquat Baig. Now that we are all acquainted, let's have a look at the weapons."

Khalid and Sunil pulled a bag out from under the table, opened it and placed each weapon on the table top. Baig examined the AK-47 assault rifle, rather popular with the militants in Kashmir who called it the Kalashnikov; the Glock 17 with suppressor and the Soviet-made Dragunovs.

"Who are our snipers?" he asked.

"Thomas and Ranjit, sir," said Tripathi.

"You boys are going to have to be very quick."

Baig pocketed the Glock, the suppressor and its four magazines. The AK-47s were distributed between Tripathi, Khalid, Sunil and Rakesh. Khalid was also given the responsibility of operating the RPG launcher. Baig then picked up one of the two cheese block-like PMN-1 mines. He noticed the thick steel ring protruding out of the mine. He shoved both mines into a transparent waterproof bag. They left for Uri after lunch. The journey took five hours, with a bit of snow and constant rainfall. They reached the Battalion Headquarters of the designated unit at half-past seven. They set off towards the LC after a quick dinner. Once they reached, the team unloaded the equipment while Baig asked around for Lieutenant Kapoor. He was led to a small sandbag bunker. There was a single yellow bulb hanging from the tin roof. Behind a table stood an officer, his back to Baig, observing a map of the area. He heard footsteps and turned around.

"_Jai Hind_, sir!" he snapped to attention.

"_Jai Hind_. I'm Liaquat."

"I'm Neil, sir."

He stood tall at six feet with a flat stomach, spectacles, a neatly trimmed moustache and light brown hair.

"So, what's the situation like?"

"Not too good. Pakistan hasn't been too happy with us, what with the constant accusations of harbouring and training militants we keep throwing at them. Ceasefire is being violated every day, supported by mortar shelling."

"Weather?"

"Very cold. Rainy. It's snowing on the nearby mountains. The absence of snow here is an advantage. When we cross over, there will be no footprints. And if snowfall miraculously occurs, the footprints will be wiped out by the rain."

"How do I get into the town?"

Neil pulled a sand model out from under the table and placed it on the surface.

"This is a small-scale model of the area between Muzaffarabad and Uri. It has been constructed using satellite images. This is where we are sitting, sir. We cross the LC from here. We walk a decent bit and then take a lift in a passing vehicle, preferably civilian. We jump off some twenty kilometres short of Muzaffarabad. That should be somewhere around here," Neil tapped a point on the model. "East of this point is a mountain ridge. It leads to Camp 9. It's a fourteen kilometre trek on narrow and rocky paths but it's definitely safer than going by road. Now for Camp 9. It's located towards the eastern edge of the town. It is surrounded on three sides by mountains. The fourth side leads to the road towards Islamabad and Rawalpindi. The camp is a small establishment. There are four barracks in one corner, officers' accommodation in the centre with the offices next to it. The conference that you are to attend is likely to be conducted in this hut here, right at the edge of the camp. Completely secluded for around two hundred yards."

"Great. What time do we move?"

"Another ten minutes. We'll drive down to the infiltration point. The distance is around ten kilometres."

"How difficult is it to scale the ridge and move along the paths that you've indicated on the model?"

"Not very. One doesn't have to go very high. Going even thirty feet above the ground should be good enough."

"No mountaineering equipment required?"

"No, sir."

"Good. I just want you to get hold of a map of the area and a compass. Then we'll move."

Baig, his team, Neil, one JCO and four Other Ranks piled into the two jeeps and set off in the darkness, only the engines making noise. The jeeps stopped after a half-hour bumpy ride.

"Sir, this is it. This is where we cross over from." Turning to the JCO, he said, "*Sahib*, please be here with a team by four tomorrow evening. Stay here till midnight. If we don't turn up by then, inform the Company JCO. He knows what to do!

"Okay, sir."

Eight figures set off towards the Line of Control. Baig was wearing a thick tracksuit and had a Pakistan Army uniform in his rucksack. The others were also wearing tracksuits. They were carrying their weapons and in their backpacks were ECCE suits. They bustled past a pillar which said 'INDIA' and hurried over to a clump of boulders, keeping an eye out for any nearby enemy soldiers. The team moved stealthily past the militarised area, looking out for light towers. They walked in single file for an hour. Once clear of any bunkers and trenches, Baig called halt.

"Neil, map! Khalid, torch!"

Baig marked a few points and areas on the map. With a lot of whispering and nodding of heads, Baig explained to the team the plan he had formulated. He then changed into the Pakistan Army uniform and fished out the documents he had been given in Delhi two months back. Assuming that he looked okay, Major Zulfiqar Afridi set off towards the highway with seven companions, their eyes hunting for a vehicle. After ten minutes of walking in the bitter cold and thin fog, Baig saw a truck coming from an adjoining road. The others fell back a little. Baig waved it over. The driver poked his head out.

"Yes, sir?"

"I want a lift. Can you drop me off on the Pindi highway?"

"Definitely, sir. Please get in."

While Baig asked the driver to give him a lift, the seven others quietly got into the back of the truck. The driver played Punjabi music all the way through, singing along at times.

"How fast does your truck go?"

"Since it's foggy right now, I go a lot slower and cover about thirty kilometres in an hour. Normally, she gives me fifty an hour."

"That's quite good."

"Isn't it? My wife keeps telling me to get rid of her but I refuse. I've had my truck longer than I've been married."

"Where are you from?"

"Ludhiana."

"Then what are you doing in Pakistan?"

"My father and I had come to Quetta two days before Partition. He had to deliver some goods there and took me along. We got stranded there and was never able to make it back across. But I'm planning to move back as soon as possible. I am sure a lot has changed but my mother and my other relatives in Ludhiana are waiting for my father, my wife and me."

Baig had a sudden surge of respect for the jovial man. Partition had separated numerous families and many had had to settle down on the other side of the Radcliffe Line but here was a man who, forty-three years on, believed he could still go back home.

"Then what about your truck?"

"I'll sell it off, sir. But only to a fellow Punjabi. No one else."

"How old are you?"

"I'm forty-eight now. But I still feel twenty years old!"

"How far are we from Muzaffarabad?"

"About thirty kilometres."

Half an hour later, a yellow board caught Baig's eye. He told the driver to stop the truck and jumped out. The drizzle turned into a downpour as he walked up to the board and flashed his torch beam at it. The driver shouted out.

"What happened, sir?"

"Reading the board, my friend," Baig shouted back. "It says 'Muzaffarabad-20 kilometres!' Baig's voice was extra clear and extra loud this time.

Just to make his point clear, he turned around and flicked the button of the torch between 'on' and 'off' a couple of times.

"Damn torch!" he smacked it on his thigh.

It fell to the ground on full beam. As Baig bent down to pick it up, he could see pairs of feet through the tyre-gaps. As soon as he saw the seventh pair, he picked up the torch and jumped back in. He was drenched.

"Sir, you shouldn't jump out in weather like this. You'll fall ill. Here, dry yourself," the driver handed Baig a towel.

Baig dried his hair, removed his shirt and put on his tracksuit upper. They drove for another half-hour before the driver brought his foot down on the brake pedal.

"This is it, sir. This is the Pindi highway."

"Thank you very much."

Baig coaxed the driver into taking five hundred Pakistani rupees. As he handed the driver the money, he also slipped him a note.

"What is this, sir?"

"Call this number. He'll help you and your family in going back to Ludhiana. He'll also give you Indian currency in exchange for Pakistani currency. Whatever help you need, you call him. And if he asks who sent you, tell him the name Baig. He'll know who it is."

The driver burst into tears and hugged Baig.

"Thank you, sir. May the Almighty help you in all your endeavours."

Baig shook hands with him and jumped out. The driver waved to Baig as he proceeded towards Rawalpindi. At the entrance of Camp 9, Baig showed his identification.

"I'm Major Zulfiqar Afridi. I'm going to be attending tomorrow's conference."

A light was flashed in his face and the documents verified. A minute later, he was being escorted to his quarters by a young Captain.

"Why are you so wet, sir?"

"Got into a spot of bother with the rain while crossing over."

"I hope this is comfortable, sir?" asked the officer after showing Baig the room.

"Very much so, Captain. Thank you!"

"*Jeeve Pak*, sir."

"*Jeeve Pak!*"

Baig cleaned himself up and sank into the soft warm bed, hoping to be refreshed and ready for the next day.

His hopes weren't dashed. He woke up at a quarter to ten the next morning after a comfortable unbroken sleep. As he drew the curtains aside, sunlight dazzled the room. It had snowed the previous night. The camp was covered in snow, as were the nearby mountains. He hoped that the team were fine. He dressed quickly, wondering where to place the mines. He phoned the Captain once he was ready.

"Care to show me the area?"

"Sure, sir. I'll be down there in a minute."

They walked around the camp, the snow crunching under their boots.

"That is the Conference Room there?"

"Yes, sir."

"What time will General *sahib* and his party arrive?"

"Around 12:30, sir. Just an hour left. I have to check up on the final arrangements. Please excuse me, sir."

"Sure. Just one last question. What about security around the Conference Room?"

"None. General Bakhshi has ordered that no one but the officers attending the meeting can go near it."

"Alright. Carry on."

"Thank you, sir."

Baig returned to his room and pulled the mines out of his rucksack. He pulled them out and took a closer look at them. Someone had taken the trouble of neatly printing 'PAKISTAN' on it. Smiling, he pulled the steel rings out of their grooves and put the mines back inside their waterproof bag. He stepped out and looked towards the Conference Room. It was a single hut. He cautiously looked around himself. There was no one nearby. There was some activity near the offices but everyone there seemed too busy to look towards the hut. Baig sprinted across to the hut, covering the two hundred and fifty yards in a minute. The door was closed, but not locked. He wondered where to place the mines. He looked at the mat on which he was standing. He swiftly moved it aside. He dug up a few inches of snow and neatly placed the bag inside the small hole. He covered it up with snow, patted it and put the mat back in its original place. He turned around and started walking back to his room. As he walked past a boulder, he saw a soldier pointing his weapon at him from behind it.

"What were you doing near the Conference Room? What have you put inside that hole you dug? Tell me now or I'll go and tell Captain Khan!"

Baig calmly pulled out his Glock and emptied the clip all over the soldier's torso. He pulled the body on to his back like a sack of potatoes and hurried towards the Conference Room, careful not to get any blood on his clothes. He stopped short of the mat, pushed the door open and threw the body in. He quickly shut the door and made his way back to the room. Near the boulder, he moved some snow to cover the blood spatter. The sun suddenly shined. As Baig covered his eyes, he caught the glint of binoculars. He was being watched.

*

At 12:20, there was a knock on Baig's door. Captain Khan stood outside.

"Sir, the Chief will be here in ten minutes."

Baig followed him, slinging over his shoulder the AK-47 he had been issued half an hour back. Ten minutes later, the cavalcade pulled into Camp 9. Hilal Bakhshi and Mushtaq Niazi looked like Laurel and Hardy as they walked side-by-side. Behind them, Colonels Haq and Gilani were engrossed in conversation.

"Hi!" said Bakhshi jovially.

"Major Zulfiqar Afridi reporting for duty, sir!"

"How is your work in Kashmir?"

"Going good at the moment, sir. The curfew and the weather have made it difficult to recruit boys for our work. Hopefully, we should be able to resume operations in a full capacity by the month of May."

"Good. *Inshallah*, with the help of the FLJK and the Hizbul Mujahideen, we shall succeed in our task of taking control of Kashmir."

"Sir, if I may say so, Syed Mohammed Ali Hussain is more of a hindrance than a help. Can't keep his bloody mouth shut. This war isn't going to be won by people like him. It will be won by the Pakistan Army and the ISI."

"Mushtaq, get in touch with Hussain once we are back in Rawalpindi."

"Yes, sir!"

"Oh! I almost forgot. Mushtaq, hand me the file."

Niazi pulled a file out of the stack that he was carrying.

"Here, Afridi," said Bakhshi, handing the file to Baig. "I'll explain the contents to you in the Conference Room."

Captain Khan was excused and the five walked towards the Conference Room. Baig walked behind Haq and Gilani, keeping a distance of about ten metres. Gilani threw him a suspicious look as he walked past. Baig's ears caught what Gilani immediately said to Haq.

"Looks very different. If I didn't know any better, I'd say he's not Afridi."

Baig's throat went dry. He caught the glint of binoculars again and nodded vigorously. All of a sudden, there were two cracks. Baig saw Haq's and Gilani's heads erupt like volcanoes just as his team started hitting Camp 9 with rifle fire from a nearby mountain ridge.

"Sir, get yourselves to the hut!" Baig yelled as he swung the AK-47 around and opened up.

Other troops around the camp opened fire. The two Generals made a run for the Conference Room, ducking every now and then to avoid the bullets. Baig slipped on a bit of brain as he made a half-hearted attempt to follow Bakhshi and Niazi and ended up twisting his ankle. Bakhshi and Niazi reached the door of the hut. Bakhshi pushed the door but it was jammed. Baig had pulled himself to his feet by now and was looking at the hut. The mines detonated. The blast covered an area of forty feet, blowing up Bakhshi and Niazi and throwing Baig with its force. To add to the fireworks, an RPG shell hit the hut as if on cue and blew it to smithereens. The team started withdrawing from their position on the ridge, firing the occasional burst. Baig was covered in blood and gunpowder. He tried to get up but couldn't. He looked at his shoe. A bullet had struck him.

"Khan!"

"Coming, sir."

"Help me up."

Khan and another soldier half-carried Baig back to his room, a third man following with the file. Khan rushed back to see the damage done to the hut and to check on the fates of the two Generals. A doctor patched Baig up.

"You're lucky the bullet was a ricochet."

"Yeah, right. I've twisted my ankle along with that!" Baig made no attempt to conceal the sarcasm.

"Don't worry. I'll bandage it. I'd also suggest getting out of these clothes and washing off the blood."

Baig showered and pulled on his tracksuit. As he emerged from the dressing room, he saw Khan sitting on a chair in the room, his face in his hands.

"Khan?"

"Are you alright, sir?"

"I'm good. What's the update?"

"All four of them are dead, sir. The bodies of both the Generals are charred. We've got doctors working on them. All the bodies will be taken to Rawalpindi immediately."

"The hut?"

"Destroyed completely."

"Was there anything of importance inside?"

"Not really. But everything inside, the furniture and all, has turned to ash. I don't know what I am supposed to tell GHQ now."

"Don't worry. You were not at fault. I'll speak to a few people."

"Thank you, sir."

"Also, get me a jeep. I need to head back to Srinagar immediately."

"I'll get it here now."

"You're likely to find it dumped about ten kilometres short of the LC."

"Not an issue, sir," Khan made a feeble attempt to smile.

Ten minutes later, a jeep turned up. Baig picked up his belongings, pushing the file into the bag and thanked Khan, assuring him that he would have a word with GHQ if need be. He drove out of Camp 9 quickly. Muzaffarabad maintained its eerie look, except that the roads were swarming with Pakistani Rangers.

"*Jeeve Pak, jenab!*" said one of them.

"*Jai...Jeeve Pak,*" responded Baig.

He mentally slapped himself. He had nearly given himself away. The jeep picked up speed as it left the town. Baig drove past the yellow board of the night before. His fingers were trembling. He opened the glove compartment. All he found inside it were a pack of cigarettes and a lighter. He hadn't smoked since he had joined the R&AW. Nevertheless, he took a cigarette out and lit it. A second later, he started coughing and threw the cigarette out. He continued driving till he reached a bend. He pulled his binoculars out of his rucksack. Up ahead, off the road and to the left, he saw a small red cloth fluttering a few inches above the snow-covered ground. He drove towards it. He stopped a hundred metres short of the fluttering, grabbed his stuff and got out of the jeep. He limped towards the cloth and pulled it out. He gave a short sharp whistle. The team appeared, a few getting up from under the snow and the others appearing from behind boulders.

"Great job. All of you. Let's move!"

"Sir, we'll have to find ourselves a hiding place. The atmosphere is pretty tense," said Neil. "Two helicopters have already passed over us."

"What's the time?"

"Two-thirty, sir."

"I don't think we should hang around anywhere here. Let's get closer to the LC."

They moved quickly, the snow crunching under their feet. After what seemed like a rather long time, they saw bunkers and gunfire. The LC was only a thousand yards from where they were standing. All of a sudden, a man poked his head out of a trench. Khalid smashed the butt of his AK-47 into the man's face. He hit the body a few more times until he was sure that there was no more life left in it. The entire team jumped into the trench. It was a squeeze but they managed it. The body was of a Ranger.

"Sir, what do you think he was doing here?" asked Ranjit.

"Looking out for intruders," said Tripathi.

"All by himself? Not possible. There must be more guys nearby," said Neil.

"What should we do, sir?" asked Khalid.

"We'll wait for them, Khalid. Meanwhile, Sunil, Thomas, Rakesh, expand the trench. The rest of you, load your weapons and fix suppressors," Baig ordered.

The digging commenced. The team waited with bated breath. The sky turned a pinkish-orange. Neil heard footsteps and made a chop signal with his hand. Everyone grabbed their weapons. Baig held up his fist, the signal for the team to hold their fire.

"Rashid, everything okay?" said a voice.

"Rashid, Khan *sahib* is on the radio," said another.

"Rashid, have you gone deaf or something?"

"Maybe the cold has eaten into his head. Rashid!"

Baig opened his fist and the team opened fire. The suppressors worked their magic, making hardly any noise against the unending racket created by the Pakistani machine guns. Baig called for a halt once everyone had emptied their magazines.

"Khalid, Sunil, Ranjit! Check them," ordered Baig.

The three loaded their rifles and crept towards the bodies lying in the snow and poked them with their weapons. A moment later, one of the Rangers fired three rounds at Khalid. They pierced his stomach. Sunil and Ranjit immediately pumped the man full of lead. The sound of the three shots from the Ranger's weapon echoed eerily. Neil dragged Khalid back into the trench and propped him up against one of the rucksacks. Sunil and Ranjit dumped the three bodies in one corner of the trench and looked at Baig for further instructions.

"Khalid, how many?" he asked.

"Three to the stomach, sir," gasped Khalid, pressing his hand to the wound.

Blood was pouring out of it. Tripathi, who had once been a part of a medic workshop in the Navy, volunteered to patch Khalid up.

"Sure you can do it? We don't want him to be injured even more," said Baig.

"Trust me, sir."

"Okay. Thomas, help him out. The rest of you, alert!"

"Khalid, lie down!" Tripathi ordered.

Tripathi scrounged through the first-aid kit that was lying in the trench. He found a packet that said 'FFD'. He carefully tore open the packet and taped the bandage to the wound. He pressed it firmly on the sides. He stuck some adhesive plaster to the sides of the bandage and clapped Khalid on the back.

"Thanks," said Khalid, sitting back up.

"Sir, we're done."

"Good. Time?"

"Four. The sun will start to set around four-thirty."

"Okay. Khalid, catch some sleep. Neil, Sunil, Rakesh and Ranjit, relax till five. You'll relieve Tripathi, Thomas and me then and we'll move out at six."

The wait was long and cold. The guard changed at five. Snow fell around the trench, the temperature dropping really low. The sky had turned a deep blue by half-past five. The sleepers were woken up.

Everyone got ready to move. Baig looked at his wristwatch. It struck six. Khalid was starting to lose consciousness.

"Khalid! Khalid! Do not close your eyes!" growled Sunil, shaking him by the collar.

"Alright, it's time. Let's move. Tripathi will lead the way, followed by Khalid. Ranjit and Sunil, you'll have to help him. I will go next. Behind me will be Thomas with Neil and Rakesh bringing up the rear. C'mon."

They filed out of the trench and moved quickly towards the rendezvous point. Far away, Neil and Rakesh could see machine gun fire being directed at the Indians from the Pakistani bunkers. As they neared the point, they noticed shadows. Rifles were raised.

"*Shree*," came the challenge from the shadows.

"*Chaar Sau Bees*," Baig responded.

The face of the JCO from the night before appeared.

"Jai Hind, sir!"

"Jai Hind, *sahib*. Let's go!" replied Baig.

The team got into jeeps and pushed back towards Neil's post. There, they had a welcome cup of tea.

"Sir, your transport for Srinagar has reached Uri," said Neil as Baig drained away the last drops in his cup. "Two of my boys will drop you there and bring your vehicle to Srinagar tomorrow."

"Let's get moving then. Very well done, Neil. You'll go very far!"

"Thank you, sir," the young Lieutenant went red.

A Chetak helicopter of the Army Aviation was waiting for them at Uri Helipad. Khalid was put in first, lying on his stretcher. He was unconscious but the Regimental Medical Officer at Uri had said he was out of danger. The helicopter landed at Badami Bagh Cantonment Helipad at eight. The city of Srinagar was almost in darkness as the helicopter descended. Colonel Pratap was waiting at the helipad.

"All okay, Baig?"

"Yes, sir. Operation successful."

"Any casualty? Anyone hurt?"

"One hurt, sir. Naik Khalid Rehman was wounded by a Pakistani Ranger. Three bullets to the stomach. Petty Officer Vineet Tripathi administered First Field Dressing. The RMO at the Maratha Light Infantry battalion said that he is out of danger but I'd feel more comfortable if he is evacuated to Base Hospital."

"That'll be done. Congratulations, Baig. Lone is waiting to take you back to the hideout. Good night!"

"Good night, sir. One last thing. The Gypsy will be here tomorrow."

"Okay."

Baig shook hands with the entire team and left. At the gate, he was met by a refreshed Lone.

"What happened, sir?" he asked excitedly as he turned the ignition of the 800 on.

"I'll tell you in the morning. I am too tired to talk."

**

10

BRASS AT RAISINA HILL

MARCH 24TH 1990
FLJK HIDEOUT, MAISUMA-GAWAKADAL
SRINAGAR, INDIA

Baig woke up after a comfortable sleep of roughly ten hours. The sun was shining outside. He felt pleased with his work. He went down to the drawing room to find Lone sitting on the sofa, reading one of his Frederick Forsyths.

"And with whose permission did you pick that up?" he spoke sternly.

"Oh! Good Morning, sir. Sorry about that. I was getting bored and saw it lying on the dining table," Lone spluttered.

"Relax. I'm pulling your leg. Any news?"

"Nothing yet. I'm waiting for the radio telecast to begin."

"Alright. I'll get ready and come down."

Baig returned to the drawing room just as Rahul Mattoo's voice emerged from the radio.

"Good Morning. You are listening to the special morning bulletin of the All India Radio. We have received news that yesterday morning, in Muzaffarabad, four officers of the Pakistan Army were killed in an attack on an area known as Camp 9. Two of these officers happened to be Army Chief General Hilal Bakhshi and ISI Director Lieutenant General Mushtaq Niazi, who were killed in an explosion. The bodies have been charred beyond recognition but some personal items have helped identify them as those of Bakhshi and Niazi. Pakistan has held India responsible for the attacks and has asked the United Nations to look into the matter. Pakistan has also attacked India, stating that the latter is reluctant to hold a plebiscite in Kashmir. An Interpol team is on its way to Islamabad from Lyon in France as I bring this news to you. The Prime Minister of India, Yashvardhan Sahni, has refuted the allegations made by Pakistan and has stated that Pakistan is bearing the brunt of having conceived and nurtured a difficult child: militancy. He has also taken up the issue of Pakistan occupied Kashmir with the United Nations, saying that according to the UN Security Council Resolution 47, Pakistan were to withdraw its forces from Kashmir in order for a plebiscite to be held. Lieutenant General Asif Durrani has been appointed as Bakhshi's successor with Major General Jehangir Qasim taking over as the ISI chief. The international community has expressed shock over the incident. China and North Korea have also blamed India, saying that this attack showcases its attempts on forcibly capturing all of Kashmir. China has reportedly beefed up its strength at the LAC in Aksai Chin. India has responded by saying that any act of aggression will be repelled fiercely. India has received support from the United Kingdom, the United States of America, West Germany, the German Democratic Republic and long-time ally the Soviet Union. That's all from this special bulletin. Good day!"

"Well, they didn't mention Haq and Gilani. Our boys took them out with perfect shots!" remarked Baig.

"Sir, you said last night that you'd tell me what happened!"

Baig narrated the entire operation, right from when he was taken to the Corps Headquarters to Camp 9 and back. Lone made for an appreciative audience.

"Wow. That sounded amazing!" he said once Baig had finished.

"Trust me, it wasn't. I stumbled once. Gilani realised that I wasn't Afridi and told Haq. Fortunately for me, their heads exploded before they could open their mouths again."

"The point is that they didn't, rather couldn't, rat you out!"

"Hell! I almost forgot about that file Bakhshi gave me!"

Baig sprinted up the staircase, rummaged through the rucksack, pulled the file out and ran back down.

"Let's see what this important file says."

The opening page of the file said 'OPERATION FURNACE'. This was followed by another page which said 'NUCLEAR ANNEXATION

OF KASHMIR'. Baig cautiously turned the page and read about the operation. Lone peered over his shoulder. Baig was boiling with rage as he finished reading the document. The last line said, "Keep it carefully. Destroy in case of capture. Do not let this document fall into the hands of the enemy or our friend at the IARDC will be in danger." He was further infuriated by the Appendices. The operation had been given 'PRIORITY' status and had been sanctioned by the Prime Minister of Pakistan Balqis Bilal, the President Ghazi Ismail Khan and Bakhshi himself.

"Sajid, pass the phone here."

Baig punched in Thapar's number.

"Nikhil here."

"Sir, Liaquat speaking."

"Hi, Liaquat. Congratulations on the operation. Well done. What's up?"

"Sir, I've got something to report."

"Shoot!"

"When I met him, Bakhshi handed me a file. The contents of the file are puzzling. I can't quite explain it over the phone."

"What do you mean?"

"They're planning a large-scale attack, sir."

"Estimated casualties?"

"Anything more than a thousand."

"It's a missile launch?"

"Something of that sort, sir. Like I said, I can't quite explain it over the phone."

"Okay. Catch a flight to Delhi this evening. Indian Airlines. Either Gurpreet or Akash will meet you there."

"What about Sajid, sir?"

"Who?"

"Sajid Lone of the JKP."

"Oh, him. Bring him along."

"Right, sir."

Baig and Lone packed as little as possible. All of their equipment was put away. Baig fixed up with Colonel Pratap to have a man meet them at the airport with their tickets. Time passed by quickly and they set off to the airport by mid-afternoon, wearing *pherans* over their uniforms.

They boarded the last civilian aircraft to leave Srinagar Airport that evening. The aircraft landed at the Indu Gangasingh Airport in Delhi at 7 o'clock. Baig and Lone collected their baggage and hurried towards the exit, where they were met by one of the R&AW's youngest and brightest analysts, Akash Mehra.

"Liaquat Sir. Good to see you."

"You too, kid," said Baig fondly. Akash reminded him of his younger brothers. "This is my colleague, Inspector Sajid Lone of the Jammu and Kashmir Police."

"Hi," said Lone, holding out his hand.

"Hello," replied the youngster brightly.

"Sajid, this is the R&AW's best analyst."

"Indeed, I am."

Lone smiled at the analyst's child-like enthusiasm and lack of modesty.

"You're a stupid bugger, you are. But since you claim to be so smart, where's your boss?"

"He's in the office. He's mean. Thapar Sir told him to pick you guys up and he delegated the task to me."

Baig's coursemate from the Indian Military Academy, Major Gurpreet Singh of the Corps of Signals, headed the Intelligence (Communications) Branch of the R&AW.

"Somebody's got to be the chauffer."

"You haven't changed."

"Where is your Padmini?"

"I didn't get it. It resembles a trash can. I've collided with other cars and dividers and dustbins and all sorts of things, leave a human, too many times. I got Gurpreet Sir's car!"

"With permission, I hope?" said Baig, his eyebrows raised.

"Of course. He'd eat me alive if I took it without asking him."

"While I doubt he's a cannibal, I'll take your word for it. So tell me, any updates?"

"I've heard that there is going to be a massive meeting at Rashtrapati Bhavan. The President, the Prime Minister, the Cabinet Secretary, the Home Minister, Thapar Sir, Sam Sir and Gurpreet Sir, apart from the three of us."

"Why the hell is that asshole Maqsood Shahid coming? Damn!" said Lone through gritted teeth.

"I suppose the two of us will have to watch our tongues, Sajid."

"Akash, that is a lot of brass though," said Lone as they sped past the Defence Services Officers' Institute and turned on to the Mahatma Gandhi Marg.

"It sure is. But sir, at least you're a field agent. I don't even know why Thapar Sir asked me to tag along."

"Thapar asked you to tag along because he knows how good you are at what you do," said Baig.

Akash beamed at him, almost crashing into an Ambassador.

"Watch out! Driving certainly isn't one of your skills. I'd like to know how much you paid the guy who issued your licence! Must be blind."

The car was parked near South Block and the trio rushed in. Nikhil Thapar and Samir Ali were sitting in the former's office, playing tic-tac-toe on a piece of paper. There was a knock on the door.

"Come in," said Thapar.

Baig walked in, followed by Lone and Akash.

"Hi, Liaquat," said Ali.

"Hi, Sam. Good Evening, sir."

"The meeting is going to be a big one. I alerted PMO this morning after your call, Liaquat. We pick up Gurpreet from Lodhi Road immediately. We discuss the points we want to put across to the brass there. Let's go!"

The party of five drove to the Central Government Offices at Lodhi Road, manoeuvring through Delhi's mad-as-a-hatter traffic. At CGO, they were met by a tall, smiling man in uniform.

"Liaquat, great to see you. Good Evening, sir!" he said brightly.

"Great to see you too, brother. How's everything?" said Baig.

"Good. Except for this stupid analyst called Akash Mehra."

Akash looked around, not taking note of his boss' remarks.

"Gurpreet, this is my colleague from the JKP, Inspector Sajid Lone."

"Good Evening, sir," said Lone with a click of the heels.

"Hi!"

"I don't want to sound rude or break up this happy reunion but I suggest we go in!" Ali chipped in.

Baig and Gurpreet led the pack, chatting and laughing, into the official headquarters of the R&AW. They went straight to the conference room. Thapar stopped at the door and addressed a nearby agent.

"Conference room has been de-bugged?"

"Yes, sir. All good."

"Excellent!" remarked Thapar and walked in.

"Settle down everyone. Pads out. Liaquat, shoot."

"From the beginning?"

"No. We are all up to date with most of the events. Just Muzaffarabad."

Baig quickly narrated the events.

"Now, where is the file? Let me read it," barked Thapar.

Baig quickly handed him the file. Everyone watched in silence as Thapar went through the contents.

"This is unexpected. Okay everyone. All ears," Thapar clapped his hands loudly. "Pakistan is developing two nuclear missiles at their Kahuta plant which, as Liaquat reminded me in January, was recently reactivated. This missile is an exact copy of one of ours. They plan to unleash it on Kashmir, cause a massive number of deaths and pin the blame on us. Naturally, they're likely to be believed since we have two missiles of exactly the same composition awaiting launch at their silos. What Pakistan hope to achieve is a nuclear annexation of Kashmir. We won't be able to send troops in due to the after-effects and neither will they. That seems a bit senseless but they hope to bring to the world's attention that we did this, thereby perhaps inducing the UNSC to take some action."

"Sir," said Akash. "Forgive my interruption but that sounds stupid and dangerous."

"Couldn't agree more with Idiot here!" barked Gurpreet.

Baig and Lone nodded. Ali looked baffled.

"Why would anyone do something that stupid? It isn't likely to do a lot of damage to our official stand about Kashmir. We are not likely to hand it over. Or call for a plebiscite. All it will do is kill a lot of people, including a lot of their own supporters within the Valley. I think there is a lot more to this than meets the eye."

"This is what I think. If Pakistan is successful in this attack, it is likely that the UNSC will force us to withdraw our forces, rather the remnants of them, from the Valley and hold a plebiscite. The people will opt to join Pakistan since they'll be under the impression that we launched those missiles. Samir, I want you to look into this person at the IARDC. I do not want any discrimination among the people who are looked into. Every single one of them. From scientists to lab attendants to cleaners. Use the phone and get some of your better men on the job. Every minor discrepancy should be treated as a threat. Gurpreet, tap into the phones of all those people who work at the IARDC. Home, office, everything," Thapar commanded.

"But sir, any mole would be smart enough to call from a telephone booth," Akash pointed out.

"That's true. Okay. We can't have people standing outside telephone booths and listening in to each and every conversation. Goddamn it!"

"Sir, we could do one thing," suggested Lone. "A big city like Bombay will have a lot of telephone booths. But a lot of them are not functional. That's quite common in India, having non-functional telephone booths. And the mole will be smart enough to call during sensible hours since he or she would, in all probability, know that calls at unearthly hours are monitored by the people responsible for the particular telecom circle. The entire IARDC staff stays in the same complex. And they all work in the same facility. Given Bombay's traffic, the mole would not venture too far from either place while making a call."

"Liaquat, this guy is damn good!" remarked Gurpreet.

"Excellent idea. Gurpreet, get your people to monitor all telephone booths within a five kilometre radius of the IARDC facility and residential complex. I want bugs to be put into the phones tonight. Only telephone booths with ISD facility. I know it sounds stupid to not monitor the others but I feel that this mole is working alone."

"Right, sir!"

"Now," said Thapar, mopping his brow. "Any questions or suggestions about this meeting we're going to attend?"

"Yes, sir. Why exactly is Maqsood Shahid going to be there?" asked Baig.

"Liaquat, I know Shahid has contacts within the Separatists. But we have to deal with him. He is the Union Home Minister," reasoned Thapar.

"What if he is also a leak? What if he's leaking information about the R&AW's operations?" asked Lone.

"He isn't," Ali spoke quietly, playing with a pen. "Maqsood Shahid, while a slimeball, isn't a leak since he isn't kept in the loop about operations run by the Wing. He has no idea that we have planted two spies within the FLJK. He doesn't know that the incident in Muzaffarabad was an official R&AW operation. He is pandering to the Separatists simply because he doesn't want another family member to be picked up. And politicians do it all the time. Look at Farhad Ahmed and the Gangasinghs. You would expect him to be on icy terms with them but that isn't the case. If it hadn't been for Indu and Robin Gangasingh, Farhad would never have become Chief Minister in the first place."

"Anything else?" asked Thapar.

"I've got one suggestion, sir," said Lone. "Could we propose the enforcement of the AFSPA in the Valley? Right now, nabbing militants and pressing charges is too tedious a procedure. AFSPA could be of some help."

"AFSPA?" Akash gave everyone a questioning look.

"The Armed Forces Special Powers Act came into being in 1958. It is enforced in an area that has been declared 'disturbed'. Basically, it is to be enforced in an area where local police and civil authorities have failed to control law and order or where menaces are too large in number and impact for the authorities to control. The AFSPA gives the Armed Forces the power to do many things which are deemed inhuman by those jobless monkeys who masquerade as human rights activists. A commissioned officer, warrant officer, non-commissioned officer or any other person of equivalent rank in the Armed Forces may fire upon an assembly of people after having given due warning as he may deem necessary if he feels that they are acting against the law and are disrupting the environment of the area. A house can be searched and seized; a person can be stopped, searched and arrested and a vehicle can be stopped, searched and seized; all without a warrant. Supplies and arms from a dump can be seized or destroyed without a warrant as well," Baig and Gurpreet recited together.

"That gives me goosebumps!"

"I think that is a good idea. I will put it across at the meeting," beamed Thapar. "What else?"

"I don't suppose we could say that the Ikhwanis be helped?" suggested Baig.

"Don't be foolish, Liaquat. You know what those chaps are like. The moment they get more money, they'll turn the barrel on us. No way!" said Gurpreet.

"I think Gurpreet is right. Our support to them should be restricted to as little as possible. Too much money is being wasted!" said Ali.

"Sir, it's nine-thirty. We'd better leave for Rashtrapati Bhavan!" said Akash.

They got into Gurpreet's Gypsy, Ali at the wheel and set off. Everyone was thinking of the results the meeting would produce. Nobody noticed that Ali was speeding away at seventy kilometres an hour. In ten minutes, the outline of the Rashtrapati Bhavan appeared, lit up against the dark sky. The Gypsy swerved on to Brassey Avenue and the tyres screeched as they turned left almost immediately. A few moments later, they entered the residence of the President of India from a side entrance. Waiting for them was one of the President's Aide-de-Camps.

"Good Evening, young man!" Thapar strode forward.

"Good Evening, Mister Thapar."

"Are we late?"

"As a matter of fact, you're the first to arrive. Please follow me."

Behind Thapar, everyone walked according to rank. They were led to the library and taken to the very last row of books. There was a long oak table with ten chairs. Everyone took their places and waited. As they did so, Thapar warned them to let him do all the talking unless they were specifically asked a question by anyone. The Cabinet Secretary Kehkasha Anand was the first to arrive, greeting everyone cheerfully. She was known as one of the very few fiercely pro-military bureaucrats in the country. After her came the Home Minister, Maqsood Shahid, dressed in a *bandhgala* with a shadow of a moustache and his spectacles on. Prime Minister Yashvardhan Sahni and President Ramanathan Venkatesh arrived together, engrossed in conversation. They smiled at everyone and took their places.

"Thapar, we'll begin now," said the President.

"Right, sir."

"What happened in Muzzafarabad?"

"It was an internal incident, sir. Some militants hit one of their camps with heavy fire before a meeting that was to be attended by their Army and ISI chiefs."

"So this was not an R&AW operation?" Shahid cut in.

"No, Mister Shahid. It wasn't."

"Maqsood, you're forgetting that the R&AW has to clear any operation by the PMO," said the PM.

"Yes. I'm sorry about that."

"Nikhil, what is the current ground situation?"

"Well, the Separatists are still adamant that their demands be fulfilled, though the two factions have two completely different views of the matter. Syed Mohammed Ali Hussain advocates the path of militancy whereas Maulana Omar Faisal wishes to hold talks with our government."

"Mister Secretary, what are the rumours of torture chambers that are doing the rounds?" asked Shahid.

"Mister Shahid, that is not something the R&AW would be aware of..."

"But you have three uniformed men sitting at this table. Surely they will be able to tell us what their bosses have been ordering them to do in Papa 2, Harinawas, Cargo and Gogoland," Shahid cut him off.

"Sir, Major Gurpreet and Inspector Lone are with the R&AW here in Delhi. Major Baig is posted with the Corps Headquarters in Srinagar."

"Very well. Major Baig, what goes on in these 'detention centres'?"

"Mister Shahid, I'd like to inform you that these are 'interrogation centres'. Each force has its own bases and centres where suspected militants are interrogated."

"They are being detained without reason!"

"Sir, I wouldn't say that being suspected of militant activity is not a reason for interrogation."

"Do you realise that the existence of these centres is also one of the key reasons that people are taking to militancy?!"

"The militancy in Kashmir is a mask. Each militant has his own ulterior motive. The big-wigs have only managed to stir a nationalist sentiment for an Azad Kashmir among others by methods of radicalisation and brain-washing!"

"Nonsense!"

"Mister Shahid, you are blinded. You are afraid of similar kidnappings like Rubina's. That will not happen. Her kidnapping was a wake-up call for the State and Central governments. The militants knew where to punch and they did just that by kidnapping the daughter of the Union Home Minister," Thapar responded brutally.

"They will pick up other children also and massacre them in barbaric fashion. And don't talk as if that kidnapping was something ordinary!"

"It was. She was freed. And she was unharmed. Militants are not stupid enough to do something that will mess with the sentiments of the common man of Kashmir. The one who doesn't want follow the path of the gun."

"You speak of militants as if they are barbarians. The Army also is killing many people, apart from all of their third-degree methods of torture. It is barbaric behaviour. The militants are fighting for a cause."

"A cause that you seem to support. And your statement is hypocritical. You are contradicting what you said just a minute back. And the militants are barbarians. Surely you aren't suggesting that the Army keep taking bullets from cocky kids who are barely out of their teens and fanatical madmen? They should retaliate with full vigour and they're doing just that. But since you're confused as to whether the militants are barbarians or not, let Major Baig clear your doubts. Liaquat, please give the Minister details of what happened in Sopore recently."

Baig cleared his throat. Thapar was sitting still, his eyes cold. Shahid was on the brink of blowing his top. The President and Prime Minister were watching the proceedings cautiously. The Cabinet Secretary was taking notes.

"After the Gawakadal incident, it was decided that alleys and lanes in towns were to be patrolled 24x7. One such patrol was out in Sopore, which is widely considered the most dangerous place in the Valley. An Army patrol usually has the officer in the third spot. This patrol was in the interiors of Sopore town and from nowhere, a door opened and the officer was yanked into a house. He was beheaded. The patrol was caught in a labyrinth of houses and alleys. The militants were intercepted at the edge of the town and arrested by the Special Operations Group of the J&K Police. They described the incident in graphic detail to the SP of Baramulla district."

"That isn't all, Mister Shahid. Do you remember the 1971 Indo-Pak War? We took ninety-three thousand prisoners. They were given proper clothing, food and housed in *pukka* barracks. Indian troops, the victors, were sleeping in tents while the Pakistani prisoners, the losers, were sleeping on a proper bed in comfort. They were not denied anything. After the Simla Agreement, each and every Pakistani PW was sent back. They didn't reciprocate. They maimed our people beyond the limits of ruthlessness. At least fifty-four Indians PsW from '65 and '71 are still in Pakistan. This is the same Pakistan which is training Kashmiri boys and men. The same brutal country with whom you wish to initiate dialogue," Thapar added.

"Nikhil, that's enough. I think Shahid *sahib* has understood your point," the PM said in a pacifying voice.

"I disagree, Yashvardhan," said the President. "Thapar is right. Maqsood must accept that. Talks should not be our priority, at least not with Pakistan."

"But dialogue is an essential aspect of democratic governance. We have to hold talks with the Separatists and the Pakistan government," argued Maqsood.

"I'm afraid that is not possible. We are losing too many chaps at the LC. How can we tell their families that we're holding talks with the very country whose people killed their loved ones for no rhyme or reason? Islamabad will not listen to what we have to say. And there will be no trilateral talks. If there has to be dialogue, it will happen only with Pakistan and only after they stop pumping militants into our country," the President spoke firmly.

"I refuse to be party to a meeting where we decide not to hold talks with our neighbours!"

"By all means, leave the government if you wish to. But I will tell you this, Maqsood. Stop pandering to the Separatists and the Pakistanis. They believe that they can win you over. You have conveniently forgotten the number of men who have died defending Kashmir. The eighty crore people of this country sleep peacefully because these men are willing to sacrifice the comforts that their fellow citizens enjoy. From Siachen to the coastal regions. From the Thar and the Rann of Kutchh to the jungles of the North East. We politicians, along with the rest of the country, must respect the sacrifices made by the troops of the Defence Services and the Central Armed Police Forces. The democracy you speak of exists because the Armed Forces give more than their best to ensure its existence. They're not paid well for it. We politicians owe them a lot more, given that they haven't attempted to take over the country in spite of the ridiculous comments some of our 'esteemed' colleagues make about them. Also, consider the fact that we test their patience but never does the barrel of their weapon turn to face us. In all the years that I spent abroad as Ambassador, never did I come across a military as dedicated as India's."

"There is no question of disrespecting their sacrifice," spluttered Maqsood. "But they must withdraw from Kashmir. The plebiscite has to be held."

"That is for the United Nations to decide, Shahid *sahib*," said Sahni.

"Very well. I'm leaving now. Thank you and good night!"

Maqsood got up in a huff and was about to walk out when Venkatesh spoke again.

"Maqsood, this meeting is highly confidential. I hope you will not act like a fussy politician and make a press statement about it. That would create a lot of trouble."

"Yes. I understand."

He left the room.

"Nikhil, you certainly weren't very diplomatic there," Sahni smiled.

"With all due respect, sir, nor was the Minister. We have to think practically. Our defensive strategies are not working. We have to be more attacking. We have given away so much of territory in our treaties and agreements with Pakistan, be it '65 or '71. And they haven't reciprocated. Had they abided by the UN's decision, we wouldn't have been facing this kind of scenario in Kashmir."

"I'd like to make a point here."

The Cabinet Secretary had spoken. All heads turned towards her.

"I agree with Nikhil. We have to be more aggressive. The government must take a call on that."

"What do you suggest, Kehkasha?" asked Sahni.

"We could do with raising a few more formations."

"But we already have the Rashtriya Rifles in Kashmir and the Assam Rifles in the North East."

"Those are specialised forces, sir. In the Army's case, we could raise a few more divisions, brigades and battalions. Each infantry regiment can maintain at least two battalions at a time in the Valley. That gives us fifty-six battalions and that too just from the infantry. We need to man the International Border in larger numbers."

"That's a very good idea," the President smiled.

He picked up the receiver of a telephone in front of him.

"I'd like to meet General Singhania tomorrow morning at ten o'clock please."

"Anything else?" asked Sahni.

"Yes, sir. Since we couldn't speak openly in front of the Minister, I thought it would be better if I brought this up right now."

"This is about the file you had told me about?"

"Yes."

"Okay. Shoot."

"Pakistan has re-activated its nuclear plant at Kahuta. When Major Baig returned from Pakistan in January, he told me about this. I felt it was fishy. Recently, Baig attended that conference in Muzaffarabad..."

"Wait a minute. You just said that that had nothing to do with the R&AW," the President interrupted.

"I lied, sir. Anyway, over there, he was handed a file by the Pakistan Army Chief Hilal Bakhshi. I went through the file before we came here. They have started work on two nuclear missiles identical to one of ours and plan to launch them on Kashmir. It is a carbon copy of the missile we possess. With all markings as well. They plan to blame such an incident on India. While it sounds a bit mad, I have a fair idea of what their intention is. They will bomb Kashmir. A massive number of people will die and almost twice as many will be wounded. The UN will be called to act upon such a situation. They may send in Peace Keeping Forces. Kashmiris will turn against India. If the UN decides to hold a plebiscite, we stand to lose the Valley to Pakistan. Sentiment will be completely anti-India."

"Isn't it already?" asked Venkatesh.

"No. It only seems to be so because only the viewpoint of the Separatists and the militants and their supporters is given media coverage."

"Nikhil, do you have any idea how they got blueprints of the missile in question?" asked Anand.

"Yes. They have a mole in the Indian Atomic Research & Development Centre. The file clearly says "Keep it carefully. Destroy in case of capture. Do not let this document fall into the hands of the enemy or our friend at the IARDC will be in danger". We are tapping phone lines already."

"This is a recipe for disaster. We cannot let any more information leak out of the IARDC. But how do we get the mole?" Anand pondered.

"Inspector Lone here had a very smart idea. He feels that the mole will be smart enough to not use an office or residence telephone. He or she has to call from a phone booth."

"What about restaurants?"

"That isn't possible. This mole is likely to have been leaking information for a very long time. Any restaurant has its phone at the reception. The receptionist is likely to find it suspicious that a person keeps calling from their phone."

"He could be calling from different restaurants each time."

"Again, the chances are slim. The people who work at the IARDC wear a specific uniform. And the IARDC is located in an area where most of the restaurants are old. It'll seem highly suspicious that an IARDC official, who possesses phones both at home and in office, is using the phone of a restaurant on certain days. It will raise too many eyebrows. The same applies to telephone booths as well but that's another assumption we will have to make. And we have reason to believe that this person will call only during working hours."

"Why is that, Nikhil?" asked Sahni.

"Sir, since we have already assumed that they are using a telephone booth, consider this: each telecom circle has telephone booths in its jurisdiction. Calls at unearthly hours alert the circle office. Operators can listen in."

"But this is all a matter of chance and probability, Nikhil," argued Anand.

"That is a risk we will have to take. Restaurants have been completely ruled out because they have a lot of customers during lunch and tea breaks. The mole will not be able listen to anything clearly, given the ruckus that is created at times of eating."

"But there are so many telephone booths in Bombay, Thapar," said Venkatesh.

"Problem solved, sir. We will make enquiries. Certain telephone booths are bound to be out of order. So they can be crossed off. The mole will not venture out too far during working hours since he or she has to be back in the office in time. So we have limited our search to telephone booths which lie in a radius of five kilometres within the IARDC facility and residential complex. Our people will place bugs in these phones. Our agents at the Intelligence (Communications) Branch are monitoring the working phones. We will have agents placed near each telephone booth as well. Our smartest analyst, Akash Mehra, that kid there, will relay information as it comes in. This mole will be caught."

"Okay. Well done. All of you!" said Venkatesh.

"Sir, I did have one small request to make," said Thapar.

"Yes?"

"I wanted to suggest that the government consider imposing the AFSPA in the Valley."

"The AFSPA? Human rights groups will have a field day, Nikhil. I'm tired of seeing those clowns in my office," said Sahni.

"I understand that, sir. But it's our best chance at catching militants. The AFSPA may be draconian but it is effective. We'll hunt the hunters."

"Nikhil, that is all fine but the AFSPA is still existent in Punjab and almost all of the North East. The opposition will make life miserable for the Centre if the AFSPA is imposed in one more state," explained Sahni.

"Sir, that is a valid point but we need to give the Forces extreme powers in the Valley. Our men are still carrying weapons from the time of the British Raj while the militants have the latest equipment from China, the Soviet Union and the United States. The troops are almost defenceless. We need to take certain precautions and I'm confident that AFSPA is one of them. Please consider it. And if you want an edge over Robin, you can always remind him that it was his grandfather's decision to impose AFSPA in the North-East and his mother's to impose it in Punjab."

"Alright. I'll think about it," Sahni agreed.

All parties dispersed. Akash and Gurpreet returned to CGO. Thapar went home and Baig and Lone went with Ali to his place. They sank into the sofas in the living room as soon as they walked in. Ali switched on the lights. From one of the photographs on the wall, Baig saw his brother and Ali beaming down at him.

"Liaquat, drink?" Ali asked.

"Sure."

"Sajid?"

"I wouldn't mind one, sir. May I smoke?"

"Go ahead!"

They sat in silence. Lone was puffing away at his cigarette, Ali was humming a tune and Baig was swirling the contents in his glass of whisky.

"Sam?"

"Yeah?"

"Before I left Delhi in January, I had asked you to do something for me. Any update on that?"

"Yes. I have some bad news."

"What is it? Randeep has an American girlfriend or something?"

"No. It's worse than that. Wait, I'll tell Gurpreet to get the equipment from the office."

Ali walked over to the phone and dialled quickly, knowing that Baig was watching him.

"Gurpeet? Sam here. Listen. Go down to 'Restricted Access'. There is a cabinet labelled 'Confidential SA'. You'll find a cassette and an envelope inside. Get them over to my place ASAP! Don't touch anything else. And bring Akash with you. Along with his portable computer and cassette player."

"Sam, are you going to tell me anything at all before those two get here?" asked Baig as Ali put the receiver back in its groove.

"Yes," Ali took a sip of his drink. "Your brother-in-law has links with the Hizbul Mujahideen!"

**

11

REVELATIONS

"Hizbul? Randeep?"

"Yeah."

"But what is his motivation? He has no religious affiliation to the Hizbul guys. What is the connection?"

"You sound naive, Liaquat. Not all militant connections have to be religious. Some are in it just for the money. Like quite a few of the militants in Kashmir, Randeep is earning handsome monetary profits due to his support of militancy."

"Where is he right now?"

"In Delhi."

"Bring him in."

"Can't do that. You see, once you told me to have him followed, I spoke to Thapar. He is up to date with everything concerning Randeep. However, he feels that if we bring him in, the operation could be jeopardised."

"How?"

"The main funding for Hussain's Hardliners and the Hizbul guys comes from Global Banking Corporation. It's a business front. The main links are buried deep in China and North Korea. A team of ISI agents handle the setup from there. GBC is almost everywhere. They supply money for terrorism, extortion and political movements to a lot of Pakistan-backed nations and groups."

"What do they get in return?"

"Freedom to carry out business in countries where they want to. The people to whom they supply money help GBC with the dirty work."

"What is the situation in India?"

"Not too good for them. Randeep is the only one who knows that it's a bogus organisation."

"But he's the Managing Director. Surely he can get a lot of money out!"

"He can't. We recently asked various agencies to look into the finances of GBC. We shared information about gangsters with them and got GBC's finances in return. Till now, they've only managed to smuggle out a few hundred crores."

"That's a gigantic amount!"

"Not if you have to pay kickbacks to a lot of government officials."

"Are any of our government people involved in this?"

"No. Not that the Wing knows of. But we're keeping a close watch on finances of all government officials."

The doorbell rang. Ali opened the door and Gurpreet and Akash walked in.

"Sir, I have brought the cassette, the player, the computer and the analyst."

"Let's get started."

The five of them huddled around the dining table and Akash started to fiddle around with the computer and the cassette player. A few minutes later, the cassette started to play. The audio wasn't clear. Akash typed furiously on the keyboard. The audio cleared up and sounded sharper. Baig heard his brother-in-law's voice and a few other voices. Ali took notes quickly. The tape stopped playing after five minutes.

"Did you recognise the voices of the people with Randeep?" asked Ali.

"Somewhat. There were four men. Randeep, Hilal Bakhshi, Mushtaq Niazi and Syed Samiuddin."

"Very good. This meeting happened in Rawalpindi. Early February."

"Pindi? I thought he went to New York."

"He did. Two of our men tailed him there. He stayed at The Plaza. He was met by a couple of guys there too. They discussed money and how it was to be sent to Pakistan. They spoke of weapons and explosives smuggling too. Randeep promised those chaps around two hundred crores for that. In return, he was going to get a free market in the Middle East and Pakistan. He roamed around the city for a few days. He signed four cheques worth a total of one hundred and fifty crores on behalf of GBC. He left for Pindi soon after that. In Pindi, he met Samiuddin, Bakhshi and Shah. He gave them more money. He was assured of profits in Pakistan."

"Dhananjay Sinha was tailing Randeep in Pakistan. These are the photographs from his visits to Pindi, Islamabad, Abbottabad and Lahore. Atif Qureshi was on the case in PoK. Randeep visited ISI-controlled training camps. He met young boys and men who had crossed the border from Kashmir. He handed them their brides, their Kalashnikovs," Gurpreet spoke softly.

"Why is he getting money from the ISI and giving it back to them? What's the process?"

"The federal agencies of the USA and the World Bank are keeping a close watch on the money spent by Pakistan's government agencies. So, the Army files the ISI's funding as donations to various NGO-like groups in China and North Korea. These groups are fronts run by ISI agents, along with their friends from the Orient. They transfer the funds to the GBC headquarters in Shanghai. The Shanghai GBC guys send the money to Delhi GBC. Since Delhi GBC employees are handsomely paid and are fairly philanthropic, the branch hasn't been investigated by the Enforcement Directorate yet. Also, unless my sources at the ED are wrong, the people at GBC have been paying off some people. The ED is about to start an investigation. The Delhi GBC runs an umbrella program in the Indian Subcontinent. It's a hunger program for conflict zones and economically-backward countries and areas. Majority of the money goes to Pakistan and Afghanistan. From Afghanistan, ISI agents send it to Pakistan via road. The money is gathered in one place and distributed subsequently," Ali explained.

"Why can't the Pakistani Army donate directly?"

"Larger donations raise a red flag. And by following the process Samir Sir explained, it becomes difficult to trace the money," said Gurpreet.

"How have we managed to trace it then?"

"We've got assets embedded in various places. They gather information for us. And since this is Asia we're talking about, it becomes easy for them to mingle with various nationalities and look the part. The Westerners don't have that advantage."

"Coming back to Randeep, we believe he is also involved in betting rackets and smuggling," said Ali.

"I don't understand this," Baig mumbled as he looked closely at the photographs of a man surrounded by others in the Pakistan Army uniform. Another photograph showed the familiar figure of his brother-in-law handing a young boy in a tracksuit a Kalashnikov.

"Relax, Liaquat. Once you and Lone finish your job, we'll close the gates for Randeep. ED has already started gathering information about his finances and assets. The CBI has opened a file on Randeep. As has the Wing."

"But what about the money that's already gone?"

"We'll get Randeep to make a deal in return for a full confession and ask the government to initiate further proceedings," said Gurpreet.

"For now, I want you to try and forget this and concentrate on the task at hand," said Ali.

Baig nodded.

"Sam Sir, we'd better make a move. Take care, Liaquat. Nice to meet you, Lone. Akash, come on!"

"Okay."

Gurpreet and Akash left for the CGO after a short while. The other three sat in silence in Ali's drawing room, their minds clearly on the revelations that had come to the fore not so long ago.

**

12

MYSTERY

APRIL 2ND 1990
FLJK HIDEOUT, MAISUMA-GAWAKADAL,
SRINAGAR, INDIA

The gardens were dazzling. The snow had melted away. Srinagar started to settle into the spring. Militancy was still highly active, squandering hopes of a good tourist season. In Maisuma-Gawakadal, Baig and Lone prepared themselves for a visit to Anantnag.

"Nervous, Sajid?"

"No, sir. If I were to be completely truthful, I'd say that I'm looking forward to this recruitment process."

"Remember to talk like an India-hating militant!"

Lone laughed, "Having gone to school with a bunch of them, it shouldn't be difficult!"

Within minutes, they were on their way to Anantnag. At Khanabal, they were told by BSF troops to park the car and get themselves screened. They were searched and their IDs were checked. They drove to a small forest just off the Anantnag-Bijbehara road. They parked the car near some shops and hurried into one of the narrow lanes. They were met by a tall young man called Jamshed.

"Jamshed, where are the boys?" asked Lone.

"Everyone is in the forest, Sajid *bhai*. Far away from the prying eyes of the uniformed men."

They followed Jamshed past a lot of houses and into one. They exited into the backyard and saw the beginning of the forest. A nice breeze was blowing through the trees.

"Jamshed, how come the Army doesn't know that the AKF has a base in the forest?" asked Lone as they leaped over the hedges.

"Because there isn't one. We've just set it up as a meeting place. You will only speak to the boys today."

"How many?" asked Baig.

"Around four hundred. Most of them are inexperienced."

"What about the experienced ones?"

"There are just fifty of us. The others have all been martyred somewhere or the other."

"What?! So it's just a bunch of rookies we're supposed to train?!" Lone half-yelled.

"Not you, Sajid *bhai*. We have to train them. You and Afridi *sahib* just have to encourage them. Pep them up."

"Where are you based now, Jamshed? Last I heard you were in Tral," Lone chatted on.

"I have moved with about thirty boys to Gurez."

"How deep inside?"

"Not very. Crossing over into Gilgit-Baltistan poses a formidable danger. We are about three kilometres inside from where the limits of Gurez commence."

They passed two men with Kalashnikovs who greeted them with smiles. A kilometre on, they reached the middle of the forest. There were lots of boys, all between the ages of twelve to twenty, sitting cross-legged on the ground. There were men standing at the edge of the area, Kalashnikovs at the ready. Jamshed spoke a few words, warning everyone to not make any noise. Baig prepared himself for a long talk in Kashmiri, a language he was fluent in but didn't speak often.

"*Assalaam Waleiqum!* My name is Major Zulfiqar Afridi. I come from the land which wants Kashmir and Kashmiris to get freedom. To be rid of the occupational Indians. To be a land of purity. I stand here and see the determined faces of all you young men. You are very brave. You will teach those Indians a lesson they will never forget. Kashmir is a prison. A prison guarded by the Indians. You are revolutionaries. Out to seek and destroy your captors. The Indians are committing atrocities. Picking up young men like you without reason. They call you militants. You are not militants. You are freedom fighters. You are fighting for a most noble cause. Allah has blessed you with the power to fight because He knows what is correct and what isn't. Do your duty correctly. Raid Army camps, draw them into forests, near streams and lakes and rivers but remember, no woman or child should be hurt in any way in our quest for freedom. Take over abandoned houses or those that belong to those *kafir* Pandits who haven't yet fled Kashmir but do not take away the houses of our Muslim brothers. Forcing them out of their houses will only turn them against us and against our cause. I would like to end by saying that if you can pick up the gun, cross the border, cross back and fight the invaders, you can win freedom for Kashmir and its people!" Baig finished his little pep talk.

Everyone started to clap. All of the 'experienced' militants hugged Baig. He beckoned Jamshed over.

"That's all?"

"Yes, *jenab*. Anything you want to know?"

"Yeah. What training do you give them here?"

"We train them in basic hand-to-hand combat and they go to Muzaffarabad for weapons training. The last lot of weapons that we got from Pakistan were sub-standard. We lost a lot of men because the Kalashnikovs were getting jammed. They were sitting ducks."

"So now?"

"Now we are going to try and get them directly from Russia. There are some of your people there. Is it alright if we store the lot at your hideout? Changez from Handwara will drop it off with ammunition in a few days."

"That's good. And who will collect it?"

"I'll send somebody. Please give them the stuff only after they have given you the password."

"Which is?"

"Shamsher!"

"Good. We'll make a move now. Must be back in Srinagar before curfew."

They followed the route to the alleys and houses quietly. They slipped into one of the empty houses and got out through the front door. Baig and Lone walked back to the 800 and quickly drove off towards Srinagar. Their journey was slowed down by the movement of Army convoys. Baig brought the car to a grinding halt as they exited Anantnag. Lone looked at him in surprise and opened his mouth to say something. Hastily glancing at Baig's expression, he decided to keep quiet. Baig was staring at a house just off the road. It was falling apart. One could still see the storeys and the compound hedge. The roof had not yet caved in but there were gaping holes in it. There were small holes all over the outer walls and woodwork of the house. Baig got out of the car and walked to the compound hedge. He felt something press against the sole of his shoe. He bent down and picked up a shell casing. He could clearly remember the time his father had brought him to see the place two years back. With a lump in his throat, Baig got back into the car and they drove on. Lone knew better than to ask questions. In hardly any time, they began the approach to Bijbehara. They were forced to go through the town because of 'security reasons'. That didn't fool Baig and Lone. They knew perfectly well that the road was being searched for mines. They decided to halt for a cup of tea. They drove through the main town and down one of the smaller roads. They bought tea from an old shop where a bunch of old people were chatting. They saw Baig and Lone getting out of the car and immediately fell silent. The duo sat on a small wooden bench and sipped their tea. The old people were staring at them. Finally, an old man spoke.

"Commander *sahib*, what are you doing here? Back to occupy our houses like parasites?"

"Shut up and talk to your friends, old man. Don't bother us," snapped Lone.

"What will you do if I keep talking? Shoot me? Pick up my son? Rape my daughter? I don't think so because your friends have already done two of those," the man broke down.

"*Chacha*, we are not here to spread hatred. Which group attacked your house?" Baig walked over to the man and held his hand.

"Hizbul."

"We are surrendered militants. We do not wield the weapon anymore."

"Surrendered or active, you are all the same. You with your guns and the Army with theirs. Our lives have become miserable because of you."

"Hey! Old man! Shut up! We are fighting for freedom. It is not some hobby we have taken up," Lone lashed out.

"Seems to be a hobby. You children have a pattern too. Brainwash young boys, send them across the border, bring them back, try to engage India in gunfights and end up endangering the lives of ordinary Kashmiris."

"Forgive him, *chacha*. The Army picked up his brothers and tortured them."

"Commander *sahib*, our children have also been beaten up," a grandmotherly lady spoke. "But the gun is not the answer. It's a very cruel power, the gun. It empowers a human being to take another's life. Your people have chosen that path for themselves. But they have not considered the repercussions of their actions. Innocent children are being picked up because there are so many militants of their age."

"One of my sons lost his leg in an Army camp," another man spoke up.

"You're all forgetting one thing: these are isolated incidents. Some officers are maniacs. As are the militants. But in the case of the latter, it's universal. The Army is also doing a lot for Kashmiris. They have started schools for our children. The children are being taken to different places across India. Places where you don't have cordons and searches and crackdowns on a daily basis. There are workshops for our people. The elderly are being taken care of. We accepted the militants as our saviours, completely oblivious to the fact that they're being trained by the very nation that is responsible for the situation Kashmir is in right now," a man walked over to the counter and picked up a cup of tea.

"*Assalaam Waleiqum*, Subedar *sahib*!" the shopkeeper greeted the man brightly.

"*Waleiqum Assalaam*."

Neither Baig nor Lone had been able to see the man's face clearly. He turned to face them as he sat down next to the other old people. Baig was stunned for a moment but recovered as fast as he could.

"You are an Army officer?" he asked.

"Retired Subedar," the man smiled at them. "You are surrendered militants?"

"Yes," said Lone.

"Which outfit?"

"Azad Kashmir Fauj."

The man laughed.

"Azad Kashmir. It will remain a dream."

"What makes you say that?" asked Baig.

"We have to prove to India that we are capable of handling our affairs. Militancy is not helping things."

"We thought, as boys, that it would. But we too wish to negotiate with the Indian government," Baig explained.

"Kashmir is legally a part of India, son. That's that."

"But Indians are out to destroy us, Subedar *sahib*," said one of the old men.

"You mean the Army?"

"I do."

"Like I said, they aren't all bad. They're as human as you and me. As for the officer you are pointing a finger at, there are bad apples in every crop."

"Who are we talking about here?" asked Baig.

"A certain Major Maltani. A madman."

"What has he done?"

"Let's see. He and his men are guilty of mass rape in Bijbehara. He has also picked up a bunch of boys, tortured them mercilessly and 'cleared' them of 'charges' later on."

"He acts on official orders?"

"No. Of course, we have been unable to file an FIR against him. But I'm quite sure that the Indian Army and its officers are not barbarians who will sanction rape, torture and murder."

"They've picked up so many innocent boys. They may well have sanctioned something like that," muttered one of the old men.

"No. I disagree," one of his friends contradicted him. "Remember 1947? When Pakistan invaded Kashmir? Their people raped and looted their way to Baramulla. The Indian Army had helped us back to our feet. It's the politicians who are the problem. It doesn't matter which politician. Hussain, Farhad, Maqsood, the entire lot is selfish!"

"That's true. We must leave now. We have to reach Srinagar as quickly as possible. *Khuda Hafiz*."

"Can you drop me on your way? I stay on the same road," the old Subedar asked, draining away the last drops of his tea.

"Yes, of course," Baig replied.

He hoped that the journey to the old man's house would be a quiet one. Lone jumped into the backseat as the Subedar decided to ride shotgun.

"You children have a lot to learn," he chuckled as Baig turned the ignition on.

"What's that supposed to mean?" Lone asked.

"You're too stiff."

"What do you mean?"

"You're in the State Police and your friend here is in the Indian Army," the intelligent eyes examined Baig.

Baig hesitantly met his eyes. The gaze was piercing but the man showed no sign of recognition.

"How do you know that, *sahib*?" Lone spluttered.

"Son, you don't serve in the Army for over thirty years and learn nothing. You two need to calm down. You boys are extremely good but there is definitely scope for improvement."

"What do you do?" Baig's voice was barely more than a whisper.

"I give information about the whereabouts of militants. To the Army, I am still an asset."

"Nobody suspects you?"

"No. To everyone else, I'm a different kind of person. Internally broken. I have lost three of my five children. Two sons joined the FLJK and were killed in a crackdown. My eldest son died fighting Maoists in Bihar. My second son is in the Army. My daughter is a professor in Delhi."

"Doesn't the fact that two of your children joined a militant group trouble you?" asked Lone.

"It used to. I have gotten over it. Confined myself to the knowledge that they were militants first, my children later. They indulged in anti-national activities and paid the price."

"*Sahib*, what you said about Major Maltani, is that true?" asked Baig.

"One hundred percent. He is a raving lunatic. Takes pleasure in raping and killing. Going by my statistics, over the last one and a half year, Maltani has raped about forty women and twenty children and has killed about fifty people personally."

"And the troops under his command?"

"They are horrible. Not as bad as him but definitely crazy."

"Where is this man based?"

"Khanabal."

"Which unit?"

"That I have no clue of. He wears no beret and the 'Regiment' tag is missing from his shoulder epaulettes. The same applies to his men."

"Could he be a renegade?" Baig said, slowing down the car further.

"No. He comes in an Army jeep. I have been able to identify the formation headquarters but his unit is a mystery. He isn't protected by any of the higher-ups. But somehow, word of his activities hasn't gone around. That has to be because his battalion superiors aren't reporting anything. Maybe the two of you could help out."

"We'll do what we can. Just one more thing before I accelerate. These rumours about the detention centres?" asked Baig.

"True. Certain methods of interrogation that don't have the largest fan base are being used. One must keep in mind that they are, in majority of the cases, being used against people suspected of militant activity. That's a good reason. Those who are innocent and are being subject to such torture have my deepest sympathies. But mark my words, these innocent people will become one of three things. One, they'll return to their normal lives. Two, they'll become informers with the Army and the other security forces. Three, they'll start advocating militancy. Those centres have the capability of transforming a man. You can stop the car just here. I stay in one of those houses around the ground."

Baig saw the all-too-familiar sight of a ground forming a bowl around a clump of double-storey houses, each with a small garden of its own. The Subedar got out and thanked Baig and Lone for the lift. They thanked him for the information he had given them. As they watched him walk to the ground, Lone called out.

"You didn't tell us your name?"

The Subedar laughed and walked back towards the car. He stopped a couple of yards short of it and spoke in a low and firm voice.

"Neither of you told me yours but I'll still introduce myself. I'm Subedar Khaleel Baig. *Khuda Hafiz.*"

"*Sahib,*" Baig was scribbling something on a small piece of paper. "If anything more comes up about that Maltani character, call me on this number. And remember, not a word to anyone."

"It'll be our little secret!"

**

13
TURNING THE TIDE

APRIL 3RD 1990
FLJK HIDEOUT, MAISUMA-GAWAKADAL
SRINAGAR, INDIA

"Sajid, get down here!"

In a departure from normalcy, Baig was up earlier than Lone, who now appeared with his eyes half shut and his hair tousled.

"Good Morning, sir."

"I need you to get ready and come down as quickly as you can. We have some work to do."

Baig had spread out various manuals about the AK-47 on the table in the drawing room, including the one written by its creator, Lieutenant General Mikhail Kalashnikov. Five minutes later, Lone hurried down the staircase.

"Okay. Let's get started, Sajid. We need to figure out a way to tamper with those AK-47s before they're dropped off here."

"Blanks. We replace some of the live bullets with blanks. In some case, perhaps seventy to eighty percent of the magazine."

"Okay. Not bad. I remember reading something about an SOG trick during the Vietnam War. It was called 'PROJECT ELDEST SON'. They were using explosive cartridges. We'll ask Pratap if there are any of those. And we could meddle with the sights. If the zeroing is wrong, the shot is going to be way off target. By the way, do you have any idea of how films show gunfire?"

"Horrible visual effects! At least in India."

"Too bad that can't be replicated. That's the weapons out of the way. What about information?"

"That's a bit tricky. Operations are being carried out 24x7. We'll pass information sporadically."

"Okay. Once we get the weapons and modify them to our liking, we pass information about the location of a single team of militants. We cannot be suspected by any of the FLJK people If the Incidents appear to be isolated."

"The Army or the State Police could also tell the media that these militants fumbled. That would be a good cover up."

"When are the weapons due?"

"Three days."

"Okay then, Sajid. Let's play!" Baig smirked.

*

APRIL 4TH 1990
INDIAN ATOMIC RESEARCH & DEVELOPMENT CENTRE, TROMBAY
BOMBAY, INDIA

The scientists moved out of the Conference Room for lunch. It was Wednesday, the 'eating out' day. They formed their own groups and headed off to different restaurants as they exited the gate. It was just another normal day outside the IARDC. But it was about to go haywire for one of the scientists. Two groups got into taxis and headed off to other restaurants in the vicinity. One scientist took a rickshaw. Another headed off towards a telephone booth. He popped the coin into the slot, picked up the receiver and dialled. A man outside the booth rubbed his shoe against his trouser leg. His colleague saw the signal and called CGO.

"This is Zulu."

"Zulu, Lima One from Trombay."

"What's up, Lima One?"

"Booth twenty-one. Opposite Cheers Wine Shop."

"Thanks."

In Delhi, Akash 'Zulu' Mehra shouted out his orders.

"Booth twenty-two. Ranbir, that's your line. Naina, get ready to decipher it. The rest of you, ears on the phones!"

A minute later, Akash took the brief report for the line. Disappointed but not disheartened, he called Lima One.

"He's not our man. Leave him be. He was just calling Kamathipura for some action. Zulu out."

Four false alarms later, Akash was tearing his hair out.

"No more false alarms! None! I want that bastard to be on the line the next time any of you give me a shout!"

"What if he's not there today, Akash?" Gurpreet crept up behind him.

"Sir, you scared me!"

"I know. That was my intention. What if he's not there?"

"He will be. I took a report this morning. All employees at IARDC accounted for."

"Okay. Let me know if anything turns up."

"Akash, I've got something."

Gurpreet and Akash hurried over to the third row of tables from the back.

"What do you have, Amit?" the analyst asked.

"Listen."

The audio came out crystal clear.

"Darling, I gave you the recipe for the drink. Now you want the calorie count?"

Gurpreet and Akash exchanged perturbed looks.

"Just tell me what it is."

"It's not going to be easy to get."

"Okay. We can stop now. There is no third person listening in."

"Are you sure? I can hear some disturbance."

"That is the problem with the phone you are using. It has a constant drill-like sound. The number, if you will."

"I don't quite understand what you want."

"I want your bank account number. We will transfer the promised amount to you through a Swiss bank account. We will launch the missile soon. It's a warning for you to get out of your country in case anything is traced back to you."

"I am almost ready. I just have to go to Kaala Naaka and get my new papers."

"Don't tell me anymore or I'll be keen on getting you hunted down by my people."

"When is the launch?"

"I won't tell you. Stop asking such questions. You're being paid for a certain job."

"I have certain demands."

"I'm listening."

"The Indian government will come after me. I want your word that neither your government nor any of its agencies will assist them."

"Ha! As if we are likely to help those pigs. Don't worry. I won't rat you out. Nor will anyone else."

"Second demand. Once I have given you my bank account number, I want to see the money in the account in forty-eight hours. No more than that."

"You're not in a position to bargain with us."

"I wouldn't be so sure if I were you. I know that you have four guys here in Trombay and I know where they stay. Try to pull a fast one on me and I'll rat you out. And I have recordings of these calls. My friend at the telecom circle has done a bit of work for me."

"What if my men kill you, or hurt your family?"

"My family is no longer in the city. And your men can't hurt me. Not if they are being watched by the Bombay Police."

"You son of a bitch!"

"Easy with the language, lady. The police don't know who tipped them off but your men are being monitored. You have twenty-four hours to do the transfer."

"What nonsense! That wasn't a part of the deal."

"It is now. I have given you the blueprints and formulae for India's largest missile and you will do for me what I tell you to do. I will ring you up in two days to confirm the arrival of the money"

"Amit, keep listening. What booth is this?" Akash couldn't control his excitement.

"Eighty."

"Okay. Well done. Naina, get the man near Booth Eighty on the line now."

The analyst sprinted over to the main telephone in the room and put it to his ear.

"Yankee One, this is Zulu. The man in Booth Eighty is ours. Grab him and get him to Delhi. An Air Force helicopter will be waiting for you at Santa Cruz. Alert your men immediately."

"Understood."

Akash turned to Gurpreet, "We've done it, sir!"

"Well done. Tell the teams to get off the other scientists."

"Everyone, listen up. We've got the man. I want all teams except Victor and Whisky to stand down immediately. Get team leaders for Victor and Whisky on the line and tell them to block all exit points from Yankee's location. Excellent job!"

Teams Victor and Whisky blocked the main road exits near the booth and Team Yankee surrounded it. An Ambassador drove up outside the booth. The scientist emerged from the booth and was taken aback when four men suddenly grabbed him and bundled him into the waiting car.

"Who are you? What are you doing?" he demanded.

"Time to go to Delhi, Doctor Raj Kumar," replied one of his captors, slipping a black hood over his head.

The Ambassador moved efficiently with a red beacon on the roof. Two more cars followed close behind. In them were ten men with automatic weapons, ready for a fight in case an ISI agent tried to kill Raj Kumar. The journey to the airport took forty minutes. En route, they were joined by a couple of vehicles from the Bombay Police. Raj Kumar didn't attempt to struggle. He was smart enough to realise that the men who had captured him were very strong. He was pushed into the chopper at Santa Cruz and five men got in along with him. From Willingdon Camp Air Force Base, he was driven straight to CGO on Lodhi Road. He was dragged into the office of Director of Covert Operations (Pakistan) and forced into a chair.

"Well done, boys! Report to Intelligence and file your report with the desk officer. I'll take it from here."

Samir Ali usually managed to look like a nice, polite and well-mannered chap. And he usually wore a small smile. Today however, he wore a menacing look as he removed the hood from the scientist's head.

"Who are you and where am I?" Raj Kumar demanded.

The next thing he felt was a stinging smack.

"Listen to me, you asshole. I ask the fucking questions and you give me the correct fucking answers! We play by my rules. And don't make me want to encourage you in case I am not happy with an answer."

The phone rang and the scientist heaved a sigh of relief.

"Don't count your chickens before they hatch!" growled Ali with one hand on the receiver.

He had a brief conversation on the phone and turned around once again.

"Apparently, you're in luck! Come on!"

Ali was joined by Gurpreet and Akash in escorting the scientist to South Block. Akash was told to drive while Ali and Gurpreet sat with Kumar in the back seat, their pistols loaded and pointed at him.

"Don't try anything stupid!" Gurpreet warned him as he was pushed into the vehicle.

"Akash, drive faster!" Ali ordered.

"You don't want me getting pulled over by a policeman, do you?" the analyst snapped back.

He drove as fast as the speed limit allowed him to, jumping a couple of traffic signals on the way. They zoomed into the parking lot of South Block and quickly took the scientist up to the Secretary's office. He was poring over a few documents when the door was pushed open and Akash and Gurpreet walked in, Ali dragging Kumar behind.

"What the hell is going on?" Thapar was furious.

"Sorry for barging in like this, sir. But we have the mole with us," Ali jabbed Kumar in the back with his pistol to make his point.

"Who brought him here?"

"We did," Gurpreet replied.

"You went to Bombay without authorisation?!"

"No. He was brought to Delhi by one of the teams we had placed near IARDC."

"Okay. Let's talk to him first. Samir, Gurpreet, I want the two of you to holster your weapons."

"What if this bastard tries to run for it?" Gurpreet smacked the scientist on the back of the head with his pistol.

"He's inside one of the country's most heavily guarded buildings, Gurpreet. I will not repeat myself. Put that away now!" Thapar snarled.

Reluctantly, both Ali and Gurpreet tucked their pistols into their trousers and sat down.

"Simple policy. I ask you questions, you give me answers. If you play along properly, nobody gets hurt. Get it?" Thapar declared.

Kumar nodded his head.

"Full name?"

"Doctor Raj Kumar."

"Occupation?"

"Chief Scientist of the Blueprints and Formulae Department at the Indian Atomic Research & Development Centre in Trombay."

"Age?"

"Forty-seven."

"Very good, Doctor. Keep talking and you might be spared. What was that phone call you made this afternoon? Who was the person at the other end?"

"My girlfriend."

"Wrong answer, Doctor."

"I'm telling you the truth."

"Sir, may I?" Ali had had enough.

"Samir Sir, you've had your turn. It's mine now," Gurpreet said.

"Hand me your weapon first, Gurpreet," said Thapar.

Gurpreet did as he was told. Thapar removed the bullets from the magazine and chucked it back to him. The tall Punjabi brought his hand down on the scientist's neck in a flash. The man crumpled.

"Damn it! Did you break his neck or something?" Thapar hadn't expected Gurpreet to hit out so hard.

"No, sir. Relax. He'll get up."

A few minutes later, the man got up and pulled himself back on to the chair.

"See, Doctor? If someone lies, that is what happens to them," Thapar explained politely.

"Okay. I'll tell you everything I know."

"Just remember we don't want any cutting off of stuff here! This isn't one of the Censor Board's viewing committees!" warned Ali.

"A year and a half back, I was being considered to head the Research team at IARDC since news had emerged that Robin Gangasingh's government had given the green signal for what was to be the country's most powerful missile. Then, all of a sudden, I was shunted to Blueprints and Formulae and Doctor Amanullah Khan was chosen to head the Research team. I didn't realise why it had happened but like any other person, I felt terrible. A month after that, I was approached by a man on the street with an offer to provide information about the missile to Pakistan in exchange for ten million US dollars. I was tempted by the offer and I won't deny the fact that an IARDC scientist doesn't get paid really well. I took it up. I was given the number of a woman called Salma Karim Afridi in Multan. She worked with the ISI. They told me that I just had to pass information and post letters with copies of diagrams. I did that. It was easy for me to make copies of the diagrams since I headed the concerned department. That's about it."

"How many missiles is Pakistan making?" Thapar asked.

"Two."

"Where?"

"Kahuta."

"Are they ready for launch?"

"Yes."

"When is the launch?"

"I have no idea."

"Are they exactly the same as the Indian ones?"

"Yes. You can't tell them apart."

"Okay."

"What will happen to me now?"

"You'll be tried in court. We have recordings of your phone calls. But that will be after we do our job."

"What is that supposed to mean?"

"You will collect the ten million dollars from the bank tomorrow evening in Bombay. You will call that woman the day after that confirming the arrival of the money. The next day, you will resign from IARDC. A team of R&AW agents will be around you. You will not try to drop a single hint to that woman or else you'll have a bullet in your temple. After your resignation, your ass will be hauled back here. Understood?"

"Yes."

The scientist was trembling. He tried to reach out for a glass of water but it slipped from his hand. He looked at Thapar with tears in his eyes and spoke again.

"Will I be hanged?"

"That is something for the judges to decide. Samir, tell the team from Bombay to take this bastard back immediately. I want him to be monitored all the time except when he is in the IARDC. Two agents will stay in his house posing as relatives. I'll arrange for some SFF men to set up base in Trombay."

"Right, sir! Get up, you git," Ali pulled Kumar out of his seat by grabbing his shirt collar.

As Thapar watched the Gypsy disappear from view, he permitted himself a small smile. The tide was finally turning in their favour.

**

14

MAULANA'S PROVOCATION

APRIL 7TH 1990
FLJK HIDEOUT, MAISUMA-GAWAKADAL
SRINAGAR, INDIA

"Sir, that guy is due here in ten minutes," Lone crushed the cigarette into an ashtray as he looked at his watch.

"Is everything ready?"

"Good to go, sir. Colonel Pratap sent the blanks and the explosive cartridges yesterday. I must say, he was generous with those."

"He had to be. Blanks come handy in situations like this. And there are plenty of them lying around."

"Sir, may I ask you something?"

"Sure. Go ahead."

"Who was that man we met in Bijbehara?"

"My father."

"What? Why didn't you say anything to him?"

"I was going to say something but I was already a bit shaken by the sight of that house we stopped outside in Anantnag. Plus, he knew what we did so I didn't want to risk telling him my name. He would've gone home and told Ammi everything if I had told him who I was. That would've effectively blown our operation."

"And why did you stop outside that house in Anantnag?"

"My parents had three children. My sister Shehnaaz, my brother Mudassar and me. When I was ten years old, Mudassar and I found two babies abandoned on the banks of a stream. We took them home. My parents brought them up as their own sons. Named them Khurram and

115

Pervez. When they were thirteen, they were brainwashed into joining a militant organisation. They crossed the border. Came back after a year and a half. One day, in March of 1985, a group of militants were reported to be hiding in a village outside Anantnag. My father's battalion was posted there. He led one of the teams into the village. He entered the very same house we stopped outside. Four militants were holed up inside. One of the men with him was injured. The militants were heavily armed. They pinned down the entire cordon around the house. My father busted through to the hiding place. He killed all four of them. Two of them were Khurram and Pervez. My father didn't spare them either. He was awarded the Ashoka Chakra. He opted for premature retirement. Nobody spoke about those two. In fact, I saw that house for the first time two years back. By then, *Abbu* had managed to get over the fact that two of his children became militants. Seeing that house and *Abbu* today brought back a rush of memories. Difficult to understand my brothers. Why would they take to arms? And for what? A politically motivated and corrupt movement. If Kashmir ever gains freedom, people like Syed Mohammed Ali Hussain will ruin everything the people have been fighting for. The exodus will be complete. Kashmir will burn. It will turn into what Pakistan, according to that file, want it to. A furnace. And the people will be thrust into that furnace," Baig's tone resonated a sense of absolute calmness.

The two men sat quietly, not exchanging a single word. A few minutes later, there was a knock on the door. Lone walked over to it.

"Password?"

"Shamsher!"

"Correct."

"Sajid *bhai*, I have brought the ammunition boxes."

"Give them to me. Where do I drop them off?"

"You don't worry about that. Jamshed will pick them up."

"Okay. *Khuda Hafiz.*"

"*Khuda Hafiz.*"

Lone shut the door and lifted the heavy sack, dropping it on to the drawing room table with a loud 'thud'.

"Heavy?" Baig laughed.

"Very."

"Let's get to work!"

Over the next four hours, they worked on the bullets packed inside each of the ten cases. There were fifty smaller boxes inside each metal case, each containing ten bullets. That made a total of five thousand bullets. A chill had started to set by the time they were done.

"Phew! That's the last repacked bullet," Lone slid the final one back into its box.

"Sajid, call Jamshed. Tell him that we've received the bullets. Ask him when the rifles are coming."

Lone picked up the satellite phone and dialled.

"Jamshed? Sajid here."

"Sajid *bhai*, what happened?"

"I have received the bullets today. When are the Kalashnikovs coming?"

"In three days. We have to think of a way to get them to Maisuma-Gawakadal though."

"Tell the man to hide them in apple boxes and bring them in a vehicle. And just to be safe, throw in a few apples over the Kalashnikovs in each box."

"Okay, Sajid *bhai*."

"*Khuda Hafiz*, Jamshed."

"*Khuda Hafiz*, Sajid *bhai*."

"Sir, the rifles will be here on the 10th."

"Okay. Gives us some time to relax. Let's switch on the radio. Almost time for the four-thirty bulletin."

They went up the stairs and switched on the radio. Rahul Mattoo started to speak almost immediately.

"Today, Maulana Omar Faisal, the APAKC President and leader of the APAKC Moderates launched an unexpected attack on Pakistan, the ISI and the Hardliners. Our correspondent managed to get a sound bite from Maulana *sahib*."

There was a pause for almost a minute before a tape started to play. Maulana Omar Faisal's crisp voice was crystal clear.

"We are tired. Tired of fighting. Fighting against our own people. These are the people who have turned to militancy in the false hopes of gaining freedom from India. At fault are a lot of parties. There is

Pakistan. Their people killed and raped ours forty-three years ago and yet Pakistan claims to be Kashmir's friend. A country which has no political stability or establishment of its own should stop trying to take over another piece of land which belongs to a different people. Kashmir will be destroyed if Pakistan manages to get their hands on it. The Inter-Services Intelligence is a fraudulent front for a terror organisation. It is brainwashing young Kashmiri boys, along with outfits like the Hizbul Mujahideen and the Azad Kashmir Fauj, into following the path of the gun. Syed Mohammed Ali Hussain, the man who masquerades as a saviour of Kashmir and its people, is hand-in-glove with these outfits. He knows the ultimate result of provocations but he won't stop them. The Kashmiri people have been misled for too long. I, Maulana Omar Faisal, wish to tell you the truth. Those who believe in the true spirit of the Kashmiri struggle and those who believe in me are requested to assemble in the Sheikh Ahmed International Cricket Stadium where I shall address a public rally about the future course of action. The rally will be on the 20th of this month, on the auspicious day of Jumu'ah. In the meanwhile, all I can say is take care of yourselves, don't get on to the wrong side of the Army or the police and *Khuda Hafiz*."

**

15

ACTION

APRIL 18TH 1990
GUREZ VALLEY
JAMMU & KASHMIR, INDIA

"Quiet now. Nobody will make any noise. Nath *sahib*, tell the men to get ready," the short but well-built Major Vikram Sharma surveyed the dense forest that awaited his platoon.

They split up into eight teams of four and moved in. Two teams, equipped with Light Machine Guns, set up a base of fire and awaited orders. Four teams positioned themselves in a circle near the hideout while the last two cut off the only possible route of escape. A company of men occupied the platoon's vacated position, ready to send in reinforcements. Sharma counted the militants. There were twenty-nine sitting around a large bonfire. He had orders to move in only if all thirty were there. His first round was the signal for the others to open up but he didn't pull the trigger. He looked around, hoping to see the thirtieth man somewhere. He counted the militants once again. There were twenty-nine. He didn't hear the whistling until the militant had almost bumped into Sepoy Rajesh. The militant had seen Rajesh. The young Sepoy ran for cover even as the militant yelled his lungs out and opened fire! The first two rounds did nothing but the third got jammed. The militant pulled the trigger a couple of times and all of a sudden, the rifle exploded in his face. The cartridge had worked! Sharma immediately shot the surprised militant in the head and the rest of the platoon opened up instantly. The militants who dived for cover were cut down by machine gun fire. Some tried to run for it but failed. After fifteen minutes of continuous firing, Sharma called a halt. The bodies were gathered up. They had the required number of bodies: thirty. There were no casualties. The busted weapons and ammunition were all gathered up. In his office in Badami Bagh, Colonel Pratap received the message of the successful encounter. He gave Baig a ring.

"Baig here."

"Baig, Vikrant speaking."

"Good Evening, sir."

"Indeed, it is. We just busted an AKF hideout. The one in Gurez."

"Congratulations, sir."

"And to you and Lone. Well done. And before I forget, Hussain is back."

"What?! When did he return?"

"This afternoon."

"Are we taking him out?"

"Not yet. We want to thicken his file a little bit more. He may try to get in touch."

"Right, sir."

"Bye, Baig."

"*Jai Hind*, sir."

Baig scratched his chin and turned to Lone, who was going through a magazine with an ecstatic expression on his face.

"Put that Playboy aside, Sajid. We have a small problem."

"Just a moment, sir."

Baig impatiently tapped his foot on the floor.

"Done! What is the problem, sir?"

"You seem to be quite eager to tackle it. Too eager. I'd rather not discuss it if you're still spellbound by the pictures in that magazine."

"No, sir. I'm perfectly fine. Just a little refreshed."

"Yes. Because feeling refreshed outdoors in the beautiful spring of Kashmir must be such a problem," Baig nodded sarcastically.

Lone looked completely retarded as he gave Baig a lop-sided smile.

"Stop that. You remind me of some creepy Bollywood side-villain!"

Lone immediately tried to look serious. Baig looked at him out of the corner of his eye. Suddenly, both of them burst out laughing.

"What is the problem, sir?" Lone asked five minutes later.

"Hussain is back. He arrived this afternoon."

"Now what?"

"We wait for him to establish contact with us."

"Do you think he will? So much has happened since he left."

"On our front. On his, there is just the Muzzafarabad incident. I hope he doesn't expect a blow-by-blow account of it from me. I'm tired of narrating it."

"That's funny, sir. Seeing how worried he is about his own ass all the time, it's highly unlikely."

"Sajid, I forgot to tell you. The AKF team in Gurez, the one under Jamshed, were killed today."

"That's good. Jamshed was one of the few who knew his job properly."

"In that case, I'd say it was smart of us that we got unmarked bullets. I think we are done for the day. Sajid, I want your take on how to put a full stop to the story of the AKF. I have a few ideas but I'm yet to think up something concrete. I'm going for a walk."

"Sir, mind if I tag along?"

"Of course not."

They walked past Lal Chowk and down Residency Road. A few shops were open but business was far from steady. Shopkeepers looked at Baig and Lone as they walked past, their eyes full of renewed hope. Neither Baig nor Lone missed the glances. Without hesitation, Baig walked into one of the emporiums and bought something. Lone followed suit. They walked into each of the little emporiums and came out with something in their hands. The proprietors of the sole furniture shop and eatery were the only ones left. Baig walked into the furniture shop and had a look around. There was nothing inside that he didn't have. One thing caught his eye. It was a long hand-crafted ship. The proprietor looked at Baig as he picked up the ship.

"My son has made it. He thought it would be a good idea to keep one in the shop. Just in case somebody liked it. Business is so slow these days."

"It's beautiful," Baig said softly.

He loved ships. He ran his hand over it over and over again.

"How much for it?"

"Fifty rupees, *jenab*."

"Where's your son?"

"Upstairs."

"Call him."

The proprietor disappeared into the back of his shop and returned a few minutes later, a tall boy behind him.

"This is my son, Zaheer."

"Zaheer, this is a beautiful ship."

"*Shukriya*."

"How old are you?"

"Fifteen."

"You go to school?"

"Yes, sir."

"Very good. What do you want to do when you grow up?"

"I want to join the Indian Air Force, sir."

"Zaheer, keep quiet about that!" his father snapped.

"Why are you scolding him? It's a wonderful profession."

"It may be, *jenab*. And I hope he joins the Air Force. But our neighbours and others nearby wouldn't be too happy. They're all very anti-India," the man whispered fearfully.

"Then it is best to go about your work quietly. Read newspapers, Zaheer. Preferably in English. They have advertisements for jobs in the Air Force. Look out for those. And take this," Baig handed the boy a five hundred rupee note.

"*Jenab!*" the father protested.

"It's a beautiful ship. *Khuda Hafiz*."

"*Khuda Hafiz*."

Baig walked out of the shop, admiring his new toy when he saw Lone waving him over. He walked across the street and found Lone devouring an enormous amount of food.

"You'll throw up."

"Not on this. Help yourself, sir."

"No, thanks."

Soon, they were on their way back home, Lone burping all the way.

"I was gone only a few minutes. And you'd eaten so much by then."

"Well, it was worth it. I have some news."

"Wait till we're inside the house."

They walked as quickly as possible, slowing down whenever Lone had to clutch his stomach. As soon as they entered, Lone ran into the kitchen. He poured himself a glass of water and emptied a salt shaker's contents into it. He quickly gulped it down and sprinted off to the bathroom. He returned ten minutes later, his face having lost its entire colour.

"You okay, Sajid?"

"Yeah. That mutton was heavy."

"You don't say?! Tell me what news you have!"

"Hold on, sir. Let me sit down for a minute," he pulled out a packet of cigarettes and lit one. "Phew!" Lone's face disappeared behind a cloud of smoke.

"Are you feeling at peace yet, Sajid?"

"Pretty good, sir."

"Then tell me what you found out."

"When you went into that shop, I went to the eatery and ordered some food. I got talking with the waiter-cum-cook-cum-owner. Big supporter of Hussain and the FLJK."

"What did he tell you?"

"He was saying that he heard from his sister, who cooks at Hussain's house, that something big is about to happen."

"We know the missile launch is about to happen," said Baig impatiently.

"No. Hussain doesn't know about the missile launch yet. No, the owner said that in a few days, Hussain's path to becoming the undisputed leader of Kashmir would be clear."

"Let's see, what would Hussain do in order to become the undisputed leader of Kashmir?" Baig wondered out loud, sarcasm flowing freely.

"What wouldn't he do to assume that kind of position? Filthy son of a bitch, he is," Lone corrected him.

"Let's wait. We shall soon find out."

*

APRIL 20ᵀᴴ 1990
SHEIKH AHMED INTERNATIONAL CRICKET STADIUM
SRINAGAR, INDIA

People were pouring into the stadium in large numbers. Security was tight. The State Police frisked each and every person who entered the stadium. People who came with flags, placards and banners were not allowed to take them inside. At noon, Maulana Omar Faisal and all the other Moderates entered the stadium to cheers from the crowd. A small podium had been erected on the cricket pitch. The stadium had not witnessed a single match since 1986, when Australia had defeated India amidst loud cheers from a largely pro-Pakistan crowd. Today however, the crowd was cheering for one of their favourite politicians. Maulana raised his hand. The crowd fell silent. His voice boomed out of the loudspeakers.

"*Hum kya chahte?*"

"*Azadi!*" The crowd responded as one.

Outside the stadium, a police officer hurriedly got out of his car.

"There is a threat to Maulana *sahib's* life. Stay here," he told the policemen at the entrance. He sprinted down the stairs in the stands towards the podium on the pitch. He was gasping for breath by the time he reached it.

"Maulana *sahib*, we have to get you out of here right now! There is a threat to your life."

"My dear friend, I cannot possibly disappoint this massive gathering."

"I'm afraid I must insist. Please follow me."

Maulana reluctantly followed him towards the exit, a team of policemen following in their wake. An Ambassador drove up at the exit and Maulana was told by the police officer to get in. The car drove off just as the other policemen were nearing it. They quickly got into two jeeps and zoomed off behind the Ambassador.

"What happened? Where are you taking me?" Maulana asked the police officer.

"Someplace very safe, you loud-mouthed bastard!" the man spat as he pulled out a pistol and knocked Maulana out. "Move fast! Where are the other cars?"

"They are going to join us soon. Fire at those police vehicles!" the driver yelled.

The first police jeep had almost caught up with the Ambassador when an RPG shell hit one of its front wheels. It flew to the side, turning over a few times before blowing up. The policemen from the second jeep rushed to the aid of their burning comrades as the Ambassador disappeared. A few of them opened fire in the direction of the Ambassador but it had vanished. An hour late, in the driveway of an old mansion in Ganderbal, an unconscious Maulana was pulled out of the Ambassador and dragged indoors. He regained consciousness after a few hours and found himself in a dark, windowless room. He heard footsteps a little while later and the door opened. A few men walked in. One of them lifted Maulana and pushed him into a chair.

"Who are you people? Why have I been brought here?" he demanded.

"Your speeches have brought you here, Maulana *sahib*. We have taken a lot of insults. The way you talk about Kashmir, it seems that you don't want freedom at all. Hussain *sahib* and the other Hardliners are not too happy."

"So it was Hussain who had me kidnapped," Maulana muttered.

"We always knew that you're a smart man, Maulana. I wish that you had been a little wiser in choosing sides. You would have been a huge asset to the Hardliners."

"Rubbish. 'Hardliners' is just a term used by lenient people. Everyone else knows that you're all a bunch of maniacal militants," Maulana snapped.

"It seems you haven't changed your stance yet, Maulana. And that is because we haven't been harsh enough. We'll give you some time."

*

APRIL 21ST 1990
HEADQUARTERS OF THE CHINAR CORPS,
BADAMI BAGH CANTONMENT
SRINAGAR, INDIA

The General Officer Commanding of the Chinar Corps was pacing up and down his office. He was frowning. He wasn't used to this kind of situation. The pressure from Headquarters Northern Command in Udhampur and Army Headquarters in New Delhi was enormous. There was a knock on the door.

"Come in."

"Sir, I have news."

"Reach the Operations Room in five minutes. It's almost time for briefing!"

The officer hurried away. Lieutenant General Zeeshan Anwar brushed his hair, adjusted his spectacles, picked up his pen and notepad and walked out of the office. In the Operations Room, every officer was ready with his report when the GOC walked in.

"Good Morning, sir," they wished him as the door opened.

"Good Morning," came a brisk reply. "Let's begin."

The two police officers presented their reports first.

"We have not received any information about the whereabouts of Maulana Omar Faisal. However, we do know that the police officer who was involved in the kidnap was not an imposter. He was SP Rakesh Ganjoo. We have not been able to find him. His house is being watched. As are the houses of a few Hardliners."

"Okay," said Anwar. "Vardhaan, what news was it that you were about to give me?" he turned to Major General Vardhaan Singh, the officer in-charge of the search for Maulana.

"We have relayed the Ambassador's registration plate number to formations across the Valley. A patrol party from the Rajput battalion in Ganderbal happened to see the vehicle. We are combing the area for any signs of the vehicle and for houses where someone might be held captive. We have a slight problem though."

"And that is?"

"We haven't been able to come across a solution to how to get Maulana out if he happens to be in one of the houses. Even if the house is surrounded, they can hold him hostage. We can't have a situation like that on our hands. It'll be suicidal!"

"We use the Paras."

"Paras?"

"We drop them into the compound at night. They scout around for some time and then storm the place. It has a very high risk element but we'll have to take the chance if push comes to shove."

"I'll get a team together."

"I want hourly reports from you, Vardhaan. SP Hidayatullah, from you as well. What other news do you chaps have?"

"Sir, what if we try to starve the militants? Surround the area where Maulana is being kept and not let any ration get to them?" suggested a Colonel.

"Ha! You think that'll work? We don't want to do anything that endangers Maulana's life. He is the head of the Jamia Masjid. He is a very popular public figure. We'll have far too many problems. Other suggestions please."

One by one, each officer gave his report and Anwar quickly jotted down points on his pad. As soon as the last officer finished, he got up.

"Gentlemen, the clock is ticking. Udhampur and New Delhi want constant updates. We cannot lose Maulana. I want all of you in this room to make his rescue your priority. Vardhaan, please ensure that daily operations are not disturbed. Sartaj should take reports of any action in the evening and brief me first thing in the morning."

With that, Anwar walked out of the Operations Room.

*

APRIL 23RD 1990
GANDERBAL, INDIA

"Squad One in position."
"Squad Two in position."
"Squad Three in position."
"Squad Four in position."

The house in Ganderbal had been identified twenty-four hours back. It had been under surveillance since then. Helicopters had been flying around the area for quite some time. The darkness gave the lone mansion a haunted look. Lights were on inside. At 2330 hours, a team of twelve men and four officers from the Indian Army's Parachute Regiment had descended on to the lawns of the bungalow stealthily.

They had split into four squads. Three were on the ground and one was up on a tree. They had identified the room where Maulana was being held. It was on the first floor of the house. The four top floor balconies had lookouts who had been neutralised before the Paras made their jump. At the stroke of midnight, the squad on the tree, led by Major Dev Dhar, leapt on to the roof without the slightest sound. Dhar identified the window of Maulana's room. He fixed a rope to the roof of the house and attached a buckle to it, which he fixed on to his belt. The other three men did the same. He signalled to the ground teams that he was in position. A minute later, he got the all clear. He turned on his walkie talkie and quickly went down the rope, the others following. He reached the window which had been reinforced with pieces of wood that had been hammered on to it. He realised that there was no way he'd be able to get the pieces of wood out. He held the walkie talkie close to his mouth and whispered.

"The window will have to be smashed. Inform the Rajputs and get ready to breach."

Two minutes later, he got a reply.

"Rajputs are en route. They will take approximately three minutes. Ready to breach."

Dhar put the walkie talkie aside and kicked out at the wood. Two kicks later, he heard a crunch. He pulled himself up the rope a bit before slithering back down at a decent speed and kicking the wood again. It broke! The Paras on the ground moved in immediately. Dhar smashed open the window and pulled himself through it. He unhooked the buckle and switched on the light. Maulana was lying unconscious in a corner. The rest of the team pointed their weapons at the door, ready for a gunfight. Dhar noticed a jug of water on the table and splashed some on Maulana's face. He came to with a start.

"What's happening now? I tell you, I'm not changing sides!"

"Maulana Omar Faisal, it's not the militants. It's the Indian Army. We've come to get you out of here."

"Oh, okay."

"Let's move it, sir!"

A harness was fitted around Maulana. Two men slithered down the rope. Maulana went next. Dhar covered the third man of the team as he went down the rope. He then put the rifle on 'Automatic' burst and pulled himself out of the window. As he did so, the door of the room burst open. One of the militants fired a single bullet which pinked Dhar in the neck. The militants hurried to the window and fell back when the encountered a burst of fire. The team reached the ground and started to move out just as the Rajputs pulled up the driveway. A couple of officers jumped out of the vehicles and barked orders. The Rajputs too entered the house. One could hear the militants cry out as the Rajputs and the Paras opened up in full force! The police reached the spot a few minutes later. Dhar was evacuated by helicopter to the Base Hospital in Srinagar and Maulana was moved to his house in Srinagar under police protection.

In Badami Bagh, Lieutenant General Anwar was given the news of the evacuation in the Operations Room of the Corps Headquarters. He immediately relayed the news to Udhampur and New Delhi and issued a statement about the search for and eventual rescue of Maulana Omar Faisal.

**

16
MEETING FOES

APRIL 26TH 1990
MULTAN, PAKISTAN

Salma Karim Afridi had got home after an arduous day at work. She was thankful that her application for a month's leave had been accepted. Her review for retention was coming up and she was quite sure that the ISI would retain her in a permanent capacity. After all, it was she who had coordinated one of the biggest assignments of the ISI in its history. Managing to get hold of blueprints and formulae of India's largest nuclear weapon was no small feat. Thankfully, that scientist at the IARDC had received the money and had long left India. Just as she opened a bottle of chilled beer, she heard the doorbell ring. She opened the door and a bunch of people rushed in like over-enthusiastic relatives.

"Who are you people? What is this?" she demanded.

The people in the party started to remove their scarves. One of them, wearing a turban, jeans and a black leather jacket, removed the turban. The *juda* on the head was opened out and the wavy hair fell to the shoulders. A beautiful woman strode to the front of the group and introduced herself.

"Varsha Menon, Research & Analysis Wing."

An expression of horror spread across Karim's face. A smile spread across Varsha's.

"I assume, from your expression, that you weren't expecting us," she said.

"What do you want from me?" Karim seemed to be regaining some of her composure.

"We want you to answer our questions. Correctly," Varsha answered as she sat down.

"About?"

"About the Indian nuclear weapon. We know that one of the scientists at the Indian Atomic Research & Development Centre leaked information about it to you over the last year or so."

"I don't know what you're talking about," snapped Karim.

"If you want to do it that way, we don't mind one bit. We can be very patient."

The rest of the team pulled chairs and sofas closer to Karim and sat down.

"Varsha, shall we search the place?" one of them asked.

"Three of you search the bedroom. Atif, Vir, get those toy cars out, fit the mechanism under them and drive them on the roof. Once you've done that, drive them around the bedroom, the bathroom and the kitchen. Remove anything that covers the floor. Sinha, search the ceilings and floors with the scanner please."

"Shouldn't someone watch over her?" Sinha asked.

"I'm sitting here, you dummy!" said Varsha. She took her pistol out of her jacket and calmly pointed it at Karim. "As you can see, we're good. Go!"

Varsha sat calmly, her index finger on the trigger.

"You should know that that pistol does not scare me," said Karim.

"Oh, I know. But everyone has a certain threshold. Everyone breaks!"

On the roof, Atif Qureshi and Vir Shekhawat were making no headway.

"Vir, if you were undercover, where would you hide important documents?"

"I wouldn't keep them in my house for sure. Maybe in a safety deposit box in a bank."

"These detectors aren't likely to pick up stuff like cloth or paper."

"Sinha has the x-ray scanner. He'll search the ceilings and floors."

In the bedroom, tech expert Subramanian Iyer opened the telephone and removed a recording device that had been placed there by Atif two weeks back. He opened the back of the TV set but found nothing inside.

He picked up a portable computer and switched it on. The insignia of the ISI appeared on the screen and a password request popped up. Iyer noticed an 'Alternate' option and clicked on it. It said 'Type barcode here'. Iyer called out to Sinha and showed him the pop-up. Sinha went back to the drawing room and gave Varsha the update. She looked at Karim coldly and spoke.

"What's the password of your computer?"

"You're stupid if you think I'm going to tell you. I'm not as spineless as you Indians. You will willingly sell your country out for money. You will never find a Pakistani willing to do that."

"Then what do you think of this?" Varsha took out a cassette player from one of her pockets and pressed 'Play'.

"My name is Zulfiqar Afridi and I am an officer of the Northern Light Infantry Regiment of the Pakistan Army. I have been working for the Inter-Services Intelligence Directorate for almost a year. I was sent across the International Border into India for what is the largest covert operation mounted by the Pakistan Army, the ISI and the Government of Pakistan as an undercover agent to help Separatist groups in Kashmir free the state from Indian occupation. The plan was to bomb Kashmir a few months into the operation. We had a mole in the IARDC in Bombay who fed information to my wife and fellow ISI agent, Salma Karim Afridi, about India's latest nuclear weapon. We started developing two identical weapons in Kahuta some time back. Our objective was to bomb Kashmir with those missiles and point a finger at India. Considering the effect of the bombing, we were going to send forces into Uri, Kupwara, Poonch, Mendhar, Rajouri and Jammu. This would be our official stand against Indian aggression. The UN would then be called in and with some pressure from China, North Korea and the LFTE in Sri Lanka, we hoped to take the Valley."

Karim was trembling.

"What have you done to my husband?" she asked.

"That smart ass was captured after the Muzaffarabad incident. Tried to scurry back across the border. Moron," laughed Sinha.

"The password, Mrs Afridi," said Iyer.

"Zero-seven-two-six-zero."

Iyer typed it out as she spoke. A menu screen opened.

"What do we check out, Varsha?" he said.

"Nothing. Note down the password. Switch it off. Open the back and check for anything that is not normally there in such a computer. Sinha, anything?"

"Nothing in the ceilings or the floors. Better ask her if there is anything though."

"Is there any paperwork about this missile thing in this place?"

Karim kept quiet.

"You'd better answer her questions, Salma. Otherwise, one phone call to Delhi and your darling husband will be on his way to *jannat*," said Sinha.

"There's something here," Iyer called out.

He pulled out a bunch of papers from the base of the computer and eyed a chip.

"That's a location-sensitive chip. If we switch this thing on outside Multan, the entire memory of the computer will be wiped and we'll be left with nothing."

"But how do you know it won't work outside Multan specifically?" asked Sinha.

"It's a yellow chip. They usually don't work outside a specific area. Green ones don't work outside their home country. Blue ones work only in a particular continent or subcontinent. Red ones work across the world."

"How accurate is the location?" asked Varsha.

"In India, it won't be very accurate. It will only be able to pinpoint zones: north, west, central, east and south."

"If we use it in Delhi?" Dhananjay asked.

"We may have the equipment there to manipulate the location. But this yellow chip is a huge problem. Switching it on in Delhi will wipe the memory clean. And since we don't share the best of relations with China, we don't have any chips of this kind. Pakistan uses only Chinese technology."

"Can you do something to fake the location?" asked Varsha. "Or remove the chip altogether and switch on the computer without it?"

"Removing it may wipe the memory. It may, I'm not too sure. It's possible that the memory will remain intact. And faking the location is a tricky job. The biggest problem is that the computer cannot be switched on without a chip in the slot. So, even if we do turn it on in Delhi, it's likely that the data will be wiped before we can get our hands on any of it."

"Call Atif," said Varsha.

Atif came down, looking a little puzzled.

"What's up?"

"This computer here has a location chip. We can't remove it. And it can't be accessed outside Multan. What do we do?" Iyer looked baffled.

"We recovered Afridi's computer, right?"

"Yeah."

"Did that have a location chip?"

"Yeah. That type of chip works across the subcontinent."

"Great. How different are the computers?"

"They're the exact same model."

"Then switch the chips. They have no barcode or any other recognition device. The chips are the only way of finding out which device is being used. We have taken all the data we required from Afridi's computer. We don't need it anymore."

Iyer took out another computer from his bag and opened the base. He took out the blue location chip and fitted it into the slot in Karim's computer. He switched it on. A few minutes later, he smiled.

"We're in."

"Sinha, start wrapping up the search."

As Sinha went through the bedroom to the staircase, something caught his eye. It was a strip of paper poking out of a lipstick case. He pulled it out and read the printed message 'LIEUTENANT COLONEL AKRAM MIRZA AND MAJOR NAWAZ ANJUM WILL MEET YOU IN THE BAR OF THE RICHMOND HOTEL IN KAHUTA ON THE 30TH. WEAR A RED DRESS AND A BLACK WRISTWATCH AND BE THERE AT 8 PM SHARP. IN CASE OF ANY EMERGENCY, CALL THEM. THEY WILL BE IN ROOM 2801.' He grabbed the slip and gathered the team in the drawing room. He handed the slip to Varsha and they had a quick conversation in whispers. After a few minutes, Varsha turned to Karim. She had pulled a pistol out and was pointing it at her temple. Immediately, all of the R&AW agents pulled their weapons out and pointed them at her.

"Why the hell didn't any of you pat her down?" Varsha demanded.

"I didn't think she'd have a weapon on her," said Sinha.

"Oh, for crying out loud, Sinha!" Varsha sounded fed up. Put the weapon down, Salma," she spoke calmly.

"My husband is captured. You have all the information I possess. I am a traitor to my country."

"Put the weapon down and we can talk," said Sinha.

"Talk? With you people? I don't want to talk to you Indians."

There was a loud snap and Karim crumpled to the floor, blood flowing out of the centre of her forehead. Vir Shekhawat's pistol had smoke issuing from the barrel.

"Vir! What the hell is wrong with you?" yelled Sinha.

"Couldn't hold back. We'll lock the house, grab her car and get the hell out of here."

"What about the body, you nutcase?"

"We'll take it with us," Shekhawat said with a shrug of the shoulders.

"I wish this chap hadn't been groomed by Baig!" muttered Atif.

*

APRIL 30TH 1990
THE RICHMOND HOTEL
KAHUTA, PAKISTAN

Two men in uniform sat at the bar, chatting and drinking. It was five minutes to eight. Soft instrumental music could be heard in the breaks between the chatter of other groups. The air conditioners induced a chill in the room. At the stroke of eight, the door opened. In walked a beautiful young woman in a red dress, wearing a black wristwatch on her left hand. A dozen pairs of eyes followed her walk from the door to the bar. The two men at the bar too stared at her as she asked the barman for a glass of scotch. She looked at them and smiled.

"Good Evening," she said.

"Hello!" they replied.

Soon, they had drowned their drinks and were looking at her. She swirled the contents of her glass and got up. She walked to the door and turned around. The two men at the bar were still looking at her. She nodded and they followed her. She disappeared out of sight just as they reached the door. The taller one picked up a crumpled paper napkin which said '2901'. They went up in the elevator to the twenty-ninth floor of the hotel. They knocked on the door of room 2901. It opened and the woman from the bar was standing there.

"Yes?" she asked with her eyebrows raised.

"You dropped this napkin. We thought we'd better return it," the younger of the two men sounded very eager.

"Oh! That's so sweet of you. Come on in," she smiled.

They walked right in. As she latched the door, she heard one of them whisper.

"The ISI do hire the right kind of women. Just look at her."

She smiled before turning around, her pistol pointing at them.

"That's true. Guys, they're here" she called out the last three words.

Out of a number of places, including from under the sofa on which the duo had parked themselves, emerged a group of men.

"What the fuck is happening here?" the eager one demanded.

"Easy with the language, Major Anjum. There's a lady in the room," said Iyer.

"Who are you?" asked Lieutenant Colonel Akram Mirza.

"All in good time, Mirza *sahib*. When is the launch?" asked Varsha, taking off her heels. "Damn, these are hard to walk in."

Sinha and Atif laughed.

"What launch?" Mirza tried to look puzzled.

"You really want to take that route?" Atif sneered.

"Why do you think you are here?" asked Sinha.

"Isn't it my birthday today?" Shekhawat exclaimed.

Everyone but Mirza and Anjum laughed.

"Well, we saw her downstairs," Anjum pointed at Varsha. "She dropped something outside the bar and we thought we'd return it."

"Is that so? How do know the room number?" asked Shekhawat.

"The receptionist told us," Mirza was quick with his reply.

"The receptionist changes at eight. The other one doesn't know who she is," Sinha pointed at Varsha. "And you don't know her name, do you?"

"But then how did they know about her being an ISI agent?" Iyer asked Shekhawat, playing the fool.

"They were expecting someone from the ISI," said Atif blandly.

"I suppose we can chat with them then," announced Varsha, placing her pistol on the coffee table and settling into an armchair. "I'm Salma Karim Afridi, the ISI agent you were expecting."

"Miss Afridi, what is this?" demanded Mirza.

"It's called taking precautions, Mirza *sahib*. You should try it sometime."

"We weren't told that there would be more people with you," snapped Anjum.

"That would've killed the element of surprise, don't you think?"

"Nawaz, relax. Miss Afridi is correct. We should have been more careful," said Mirza.

"Sorry, sir."

"So, what is it that you're here to tell me?" asked Varsha.

"The missiles are ready for launch. Doctor Khan and his team have surpassed themselves. The missiles have a self-destruct mechanism in case things go wrong, though I personally feel it is a needless feature. Who is going to stop the launch? Nobody even knows about it," Mirza explained.

"Except those who have to," pointed out Varsha. "What is the range?"

"Somewhere between two hundred to five hundred kilometres," said Anjum. "The main target is Srinagar. If Srinagar falls, the Valley will fall. As it should have in 1947."

"*Inshallah*, that is what will happen," said Varsha. "But tell me, why exactly were we supposed to meet today?"

"We were told that you may attend the launch. That was the main reason for this meeting. You will be in the control room and everyone else, including the two of us, will be in the Viewing Gallery," Mirza's chest puffed up proudly.

"When is the launch?"

"On the 11th of May."

"Okay. I will see you then," Varsha got up from her chair.

Mirza and Anjum followed suit and said a quick good night. Anjum's gaze lingered on her before she quickly slammed the door in his face.

"Okay. Show's over. Our work here is done. For now. We leave for Delhi immediately and get the rest of the plan in place."

**

17

THE FALLEN

The month of May began. The chilly winds were replaced by the occasional breeze in the evenings as summer finally hit the Valley. The heat on the militants however, had been on for quite some time. The Azad Kashmir Fauj had been decimated in major operations all over the Valley. All that was left of what had once been the second largest militant force in the Indian subcontinent was a bunch of rookies and the two commanders: Zulfiqar Afridi and Sajid Lone. They had been kept on their toes for the last couple of weeks. Security all over Srinagar had become a little lax. The Counter-Insurgency operations had made the security forces a little complacent. They believed that no terror outfit would dare to pull off anything. Lieutenant General Anwar however, was not willing to relax even the slightest rule of discipline in his area of command. He knew that the militants from other groups were cunning enough to strike at a time when the security forces were at their weakest. On the 5th of May, Baig and Lone got a call from Hussain. He wanted to meet them. The meeting place was Hussain's house in Hyderpora.

"Sajid," Baig called out.

"Yes, sir?"

"I want you to take your service revolver and one more weapon. Take as many bullets as you can."

"Are you thinking of finishing Hussain off in an encounter?"

"No, much as I'd like to. I have this feeling that we may have some trouble. And wear trousers please. I need you to be able to run if need be."

Baig tucked his Walther inside his trousers and strapped the Glock to his left ankle.

"Ready? Let's go!"

Just as Lone opened the door, one of the satellite phones rang. Baig walked back to the drawing room and picked it up.

"Hello," he said.

"Major, we will have to change the meeting place. Reach the Kashmir Silk Factory in Rajbagh within half an hour," said Hussain.

"Why the sudden change, Hussain *sahib*?"

"Need some fresh air."

"Okay. We'll be there," Baig disconnected the call as suddenly as it had come. "Sajid, pack all of your belongings. Each and every thing you own in this place. Don't ask any questions!"

Baig picked up the Motorola and called Colonel Pratap.

"Sir, good morning. Baig speaking."

"Hi. What happened? Weren't you supposed to be meeting Hussain right now?"

"He's moved the meeting place to a certain Kashmir Silk Factory in Rajbagh. I need you to do me a favour, sir."

"Tell me."

"I'm packing up all the stuff Lone and I have here. I want you to send a team to take all of it to Badami Bagh immediately. Second, I need you to send word to the main gate of Badami Bagh for Lone and me to be let inside in case we turn up. Lastly, please get that factory surrounded. I have a feeling that things may go wrong. But tell the teams to move in only when Hussain and his men have pulled something."

"I'll see what I can do."

"Thank you, sir."

The receiver at the other end clicked and Baig jumped into action. He threw all his stuff together. All the sensitive documents he had were hidden in the car. Within ten minutes, he and Lone had all of their belongings kept in the drawing room. The drive to Rajbagh was a cheerful one, Lone cracking all the jokes he could about the traffic and the Separatists. They took some time to navigate through the numerous factories in Rajbagh. Baig quickly realised that this was a more modernised area than the Old City. The people here were more educated and believed in sending their kids to school. The Kashmir Silk Factory was in a slightly secluded part of Rajbagh. A cloud of dust flew up as Lone turned into the premises. Hussain was standing near a rundown building with a caved-in roof, waiting for them. There were about ten young men standing in spots near Hussain with Kalashnikovs in their hands. Two vehicles stood nearby. Lone stopped the car next to them.

"Hussain *sahib*, *Assalaam Waleiqum*," Baig said cheerfully.

"That smile is a little disconcerting, Major."

"And why is that?"

"Maybe because I expected you to be mourning the loss of the many boys from the AKF. The military wing of the FLJK is finished. You and Sajid, apart from these ten boys, are the only remaining members of what was once a formidable force," Hussain sounded angry.

The ten youngsters raised their Kalashnikovs and pointed them at Baig and Lone. Lone turned his head towards Baig. The latter's eyelids twitched and Lone turned to face Hussain again. Baig's hand entered his shirt pocket. One of the men cocked his Kalashnikov. Hussain held his hand up. Baig hastily pulled his hand out of the pocket and pulled out a stick of bubble gum. He pulled a piece out and popped it into his mouth before addressing Hussain.

"I don't like the tone you're taking. Nor do I like what you're implying."

"And what do you think I am implying?"

"I think that you think that Sajid and I conspired to finish off the AKF!"

"I must admit, I'm impressed by how smart you are, Major."

"And what evidence do you have of such a plot having been conceived?" asked Lone.

"The AKF has been around for quite some time. Yasir Meer and Farooq Malik were the real brains behind the entire concept. Yasir was a young boy when he came to me, the most powerful leader in Kashmir, with the idea. He developed it along with Farooq. They brought the AKF into limelight that only the Hizbul Mujahideen had experienced. They got arms training in Pakistan. A well-structured force fell apart almost as soon as you entered the frame."

"Well, have you considered the fact that Yasir was arrested and Farooq killed?" asked Baig.

"To tell you the truth, I have. And I just cannot get my head around the fact that yet again, it was only after your arrival did things go downhill. Yasir was on the police radar, yes. But how did the Army know where he was going to be?"

"In that respect, I was only told of a general location: Sopore. I was not aware of the house he would go to, what vehicle he would travel in and how many men were with him."

"But Sajid knew all those things. Recently, when I bribed that police officer Rakesh Ganjoo to kidnap Maulana Omar Faisal, we had a chat. Turns out, he was posted in Sopore Police Station at a time when a young boy from one of the nearby schools was recruited by the police to finish off the Kashmir Mujahideen. This boy later went on to join the police force. He is standing right next to you, Major."

Lone stared unflinchingly at Hussain, his eyes alive with fire. Hussain glanced at him before continuing.

"He is the spy. He is the mole of the police."

"I must admit that you are quite the genius, Hussain *sahib*. Can we talk alone for a moment?"

"Come."

Hussain put an arm around Baig's shoulder as they walked away from Lone, who was facing ten Kalashnikov barrels.

"I could never have guessed that he is a spy, Hussain *sahib*."

"Don't blame yourself. He fooled all of us."

"I think one more person did that."

"Who?"

"Me. Major Liaquat Baig, Indian Army."

In a swift move, Baig pulled out the P1 and fired at Hussain, who fell to the ground. His ten guards were taken aback.

"Sajid, run for it!" Baig yelled as he took a shot at one of the men.

The men opened fire. Lone rolled aside and took cover behind one of the cars, taking shots at them from behind it. As he reloaded his revolver, he heard steps. He swung himself to the side and caught one of the militants unawares. Before the man could recover, a bullet had gone through his forehead. Suddenly, Lone was thrown against the car and a giant of a man rushed at him. Lone, at over six feet tall, was no pixie, but the giant was almost a different species. He slammed Lone's head against the car door. Lone slumped against the door and the giant landed a hefty leg on his chest. Blood started to ooze out of his nose. The giant caught him by the legs and pulled him aside. He had a massive grin on his face as he tried to kick out at Lone's crotch. The injured Inspector summoned all his energy and heaved his body out of the way. The giant seemed angry with the missed kick and grabbed his Kalashnikov, which was lying on the bonnet of one of the cars. Lone made a grab for it. Two loud bangs later, the giant fell on top of him. Smoke issued from the barrel of his P1 as Baig held his stance.

*

MAY 6ᵀᴴ 1990
CHINAR CORPS WAR MEMORIAL, BADAMI BAGH CANTONMENT
SRINAGAR, INDIA

It was a murky morning. A large number of officers and men had assembled at the War Memorial. The casket, draped in the Tricolour, was placed on an elevated platform. Lieutenant General Anwar marched forward and placed a wreath on it. Senior army and police officers followed suit. They were followed by two men in black suits. The last person to lay a wreath on the casket was a tall officer. His chin looked stiff and his eyes reflected a fierce resolve. They lingered on the name on the casket for a brief moment. He saluted his fallen comrade and fell back, taking his place next to the suited duo. The casket was carried away into a waiting helicopter which took off immediately, heading for Sopore. Slowly, the parties dispersed. Only the officer stayed back. It started to rain heavily but he just sat on the steps. As the rain came to a halt, an Ambassador drew up across the road. One of the suited men got out and beckoned the officer over.

"What?" Baig's tone was as cold as the rain and as snappy as the wind.

"You're going to the hospital. Come on!" said Ali.

"Leave me alone, Sam!"

"I know you want to vent. Do that tomorrow, will you? The doctors want you to have a full night's rest. Just one sedative. I promise."

"Fine! Just one."

At 92 Base Hospital, Baig was sedated. Ali stood in front of him, a hand on his shoulder.

"Sam, his pockets. Check Hussain's pockets," Baig mumbled before his eyes closed.

*

Baig's eyes opened suddenly. He looked at the clock on his bedside table. It was half-past five in the morning. He freshened up and sneaked up to the hospital gym. He had run five kilometres on the treadmill when the Hospital Commandant walked in.

"Major Baig, what in the name of God are you doing?"

"Running, sir."

"Stop that at once! We're going back to your room. Immediately!"

Baig reluctantly stopped running and mopped his sweaty face.

"Who'd think you chaps have ten years of service? Behaving like stubborn brats! Come on, move it!"

As they walked down the stairs, Baig kept an eye out for something that looked out of place.

"Sir, where's Hussain?"

"Ha! Wouldn't you like to know! Inside!"

The Commandant pushed open the room door and Baig walked in.

"You'd better get out of those sweaty clothes. And lie down, else I'll give you a stronger sedative."

Baig knew the grizzled Commandant wasn't joking. He bathed and quickly got into bed.

"The room will be under guard. Don't even think of sneaking out again!"

Baig lay in bed for a long time, thinking of the last few days. At 9, Ali and Thapar dropped in.

"I should've opened fire earlier."

"You had to wait till you had a clear shot. You tried."

"He went down like a true hero, Liaquat."

"Look on the bright side..." began Thapar.

"There's a bright side to this? An officer is dead, sir. Where the hell is the bright side?" Baig snapped.

"The operation…"

"To hell with the operation!"

"Look, I understand you're upset…"

"You're damn right! But as long as you're happy, who cares, right?"

Thapar's face hardened and his voice was icy when he spoke.

"Things happen, Liaquat. They aren't always in our control. This is one of those things. As I was saying: Operation Blazing Snow is a success…"

"Bullshit! If the Wing thinks it can mount similar operations in the future, it should keep in mind the number of Sajid Lones that are likely to die."

"Are you done?"

"Not yet. I want to see Hussain!"

"I'm going to have to think a lot before letting you into the same room as him."

A few hours later, as the skies over Srinagar turned a pinkish orange, Baig quickly walked down the steps to the basement of Base Hospital. The entire corridor was brightly lit and commandos from the Parachute Regiment were lined up on either side. One door was wide open and Baig could see shadows moving around. A minute later, the Commandant and Lieutenant General Anwar came out of the room. They walked down the corridor towards Baig. He snapped to attention and saluted.

"At ease," said Anwar. "You must be Baig. I'm Zeeshan," he smilingly extended his hand.

Baig shook it firmly.

"Good Evening, sir."

"Hard nut to crack, your friend Hussain," Anwar remarked.

"I'm hoping I can be of some help there, sir."

"Be careful, Baig. I don't want him too angry. His blood pressure shouldn't go through the roof," the Commandant warned Baig.

"Understood, sir."

"Good. We'll leave you to it," Anwar patted him on the back and walked off with the Commandant.

Baig entered the room and found Hussain lying on the bed, his hands and legs bound together.

"Good Evening, Hussain."

"Who is it now? I tell you, I'm not giving you any information."

"I know you won't, Hussain. I was hoping you'd have a small chat with me though."

"Oh, it's you. You swine!"

"Takes one to know one, I suppose," Baig smiled.

"Who are you?"

"I introduced myself to you. Maybe you don't remember. I'm Major Liaquat Khaleel Baig of the Indian Army," Baig placed emphasis on 'Indian'.

"I should have known. You Indians are just a bunch of assholes. I should have seen it coming. It was you!"

"Relax, Hussain. I had help. From that brave man called Sajid Lone. From you. You gave me titbits of information to pass on to my superiors. Thank you."

"It must have been you who hit Muzaffarabad too."

"You're smart."

"And you're a Muslim. You betrayed your own brothers. I bet you're from Delhi or somewhere."

"Actually, that is incorrect. I'm from Bijbehara. I'm a Kashmiri Muslim," Baig emphasised upon 'Kashmiri' this time.

"Aren't you ashamed of yourself? We are fighting for freedom! You have fallen on the wayward path of those who believe that India is right."

"Don't try that freedom bullshit of yours on me. I know what you want. You are a power-hungry and selfish fool! Your lust for power has reached levels of insanity. And tell me one thing, if you hate India so much, why did you stand for election to the State Assembly thrice? Let me remind you that you are still an MLA, Hussain. You're being paid your salary because of Indian tax-payers. You want your red-beaconed vehicle and your police protection but you still want to raise hollow cries of *'Azadi'* and *'Pakistan Zindabad'* from Lal Chowk. Doesn't take a genius to figure out who would fit the definition of 'hypocrite', does it?"

"You wait and watch the fun, Baig! I'll be set free by the courts and then you'll have nowhere to run. I'll kill you with my bare hands and there will be no one to witness it, which is a little sad."

"Hey, look around you," Baig said in mock surprise. "There's no one here. Why don't you try killing me? Oh, wait. Your hands and legs are chained. Sad!"

"There is still time. Join me and my men. We will shield you from the Indians. You can be a great asset to the FLJK."

"You just don't get it, do you? I didn't don the uniform because I needed a job. I donned it because I take pride in being an Indian. India is my country. And to me, nothing matters more than upholding the pride of the Tricolour. It's not just about being patriotic, which you claim to be. It's about having the right ideas. It's about having the right beliefs. The belief that your nation has done something for you and it's time for you to give back to it. That is why I donned the uniform. And let me remind you that had it not been for the Indian Army's intervention in 1947, you'd probably have been reduced to something non-existent. Another one of the dead bodies that lay all the way up to Srinagar."

"You and I are not very different. We are both proud of our lands."

"No. You have ulterior motives. You want power, you want control. Under you, a place will burn and crumble to ash. Nothing will be left of it."

"I don't understand why Kashmiris like you exist."

"We exist to maintain the balance. The balance that needs to be maintained to level things out between you, your pro-freedom friends and the *Aawam* of Kashmir, the common man who doesn't want to think of who will be the next on to cross the border and pick up a weapon or who will be the next pot-smoking, stone-pelting teenager on the streets."

"The voice of the common Kashmiri has been suppressed by your Army and your nation. You have picked up innocent Kashmiris and thrown them into prison on the basis of trumped-up charges. I am the voice of the common Kashmiri. I know what the common man wants and I will ensure that his demands are fulfilled. And tell me, why shouldn't we pick up the gun and pelt stones?"

"Picking up a weapon and pelting stones doesn't give you anything, unless you count satisfaction, that too briefly. You have brainwashed people. Radicalisation has led to their transformation into fanatics. You have picked them up at their weakest, bribed them to throw stones at vehicles and personnel of the security forces and made them like yourself. Young kids in Kashmir are doing drugs. You are responsible for the fact that sole bread-winners of families have been detained. These families have no money to buy food. People are picking up weapons because once the bread-winners of their families were gone, there was no money. And why did those bread-winners disappear? Because the clown called Syed Mohammed Ali Hussain decided to act like a fucking mascot for Syed Samiuddin and Pakistan. He decided to sit in the sanctity of his home in the safe haven of Hyderpora and incite people and lure them with the hollow promises of money and fame. You will go down in history as someone who should never have been born! The common Kashmiri Muslim's image has been tarnished by people like you. Muslims and Pandits used to be like brothers. People like you encouraged like-minded fanatics to drive a wedge between them. The common Kashmiri Muslim who refused to agree with your ideology was harassed, threatened and beaten by militants who had your hand on their shoulders. And because of that, people are under the impression that all Kashmiri Muslims are bad! That the entire lot is filled with religious fanatics, Separatists and militants. Remember one thing, you are one of the largest blotches on the history of Kashmir. There will come a day when people stand at Lal Chowk and shout 'Syed Mohammed Ali Hussain *Murdabad*'! Oh no! They won't. You want to know why? Because you're such an incredibly idiotic piece of shit that they'll have forgotten your fucking name!"

Hussain tried to grab hold of Baig but struggled to even get up as the chains restrained him. Throwing him one last look of deep disgust, Baig stormed out of the room, bumping into Ali as he did.

"I was just about to come and see you, Liaquat."

"What's up?"

"The recording bug was analysed. We heard a few things."

"Yes?" Baig raised his eyebrows.

"The two of you conversing, then a gunshot, followed by a lot of gunfire after which a car door was opened and a satellite phone was dialled. Hussain said just four words."

"What?"

"'Take care of him!'"

"Did you manage to figure out the number?"

"The Signals branch is working on it in the Corps Headquarters."

"You're going to ask Hussain about it?"

"I'll leave that to the interrogators. A special prison cell is being constructed inside the Cantonment. Hussain will be moved there in a couple of days."

"Good. What do I do now?"

"You stay put in Srinagar for a few days. Inside the Cantonment. On the 29th, you fly out to Delhi. Your paperwork will be finished by then. All you have to do is sign a few documents, finish your psychological and medical evaluations and you'll be on your way out of the Wing."

"Where am I getting posted?"

"What do you feel about Binnaguri?"

"In Bengal?"

"Do you know any other Binnaguris?"

"It's a decent place. Hell, any posting will seem like a picnic after this one. So yeah, sure!"

"Good."

"What about those missiles?"

"Well, we sent a team to Pakistan under Varsha. They captured the scientist's contact, who also happens to be the wife of the man you were, until yesterday, impersonating. They got information from her and moved to Kahuta. Varsha impersonated her and got in touch with two ISI officers. She is going, along with the rest of the team, for the missile launch on the 11th."

"And what is our course of action in that regard?"

"She goes with her team, deactivates those missiles and gets out of there."

"You make it sound like a walk in the park, Samir."

"We're sending Gurpreet and Akash as support in case things go haywire."

"Let's hope they don't. There is one more thing that I wanted to discuss with you though."

"Yeah?"

"Can you look into an officer called Major Maltani around Anantnag?"

"Why?"

"I have information from a source about him. He's a maniac. Responsible for rape, murder and disappearances in Anantnag."

"Official status?"

"Someone is turning a blind eye towards him. Has to be his Commanding Officer. And if the CO doesn't report it, Brigade and Division aren't going to take any action, right?"

"Is your source reliable?"

"Do you trust my father, Samir?"

"The question seems a little out of the blue but yes, I do."

"Then the information is correct."

"Wait a minute. You met him?"

"Bumped into him while returning from the Anantnag FLJK rally."

"Did he recognise you?"

"No. He's never seen me with a full beard."

"Okay."

"You think you could tell Thapar to let me off for a few days so I can go and meet *Ammi-Abbu*?"

"He's still a bit pissed off at the way you spoke to him but I think I can get him to agree."

"Don't cross the line, Sam. A professional relationship should always stay professional."

"You're a true bastard, you are. You're truly your brother's brother," Ali mock-punched him.

"Thanks, Sam. Let's go get something to eat. I'm starving."

**

18

BOOM!

MAY 11TH 1990
KAHUTA, PAKISTAN

"Nervous?"

"Not really. Just want to get it over with."

"This is your voice transmitter. Its receiver is in the satellite phone inside your purse. I'll be outside the perimeter with Akash. The rest of the team will be in the compound. In case you think we need to pull out earlier, say the code loud and clear. I'll blow up the cavalcade. I may do that anyway, just for the fun of it. Thank heavens for those toy cars."

"Are the others ready?"

"They're in position on the highway. They'll stop the catering van and reach the place."

"Security?"

"Atif and Vir went scouting. Not a lot. That surprises me. But we don't know anything about men in basements or underground bunkers."

"Thanks. You just made me a lot more confident."

"Will you relax, Varsha? Get the job done inside the laboratories and I'll do mine with the IEDs."

"Okay."

Varsha got into a rented Mitsubishi Mirage and left the Richmond. She noticed a catering van behind her as she turned on to the highway. She accelerated and the van was soon out of sight. As she approached her destination, the van went past. Both indicators flashed thrice. Half an hour later, she turned left onto a path off the highway. She sped through a tunnel, turned left at its exit and drove through the gates of Kahuta Research Laboratories. She was met by a young scientist.

"Good Evening, ma'am."

"*Assalaam Waleiqum.*"

"Doctor Khan will meet you in ten minutes. I'll take to the place where you'll be sitting."

"And where is that?"

"Near the launch pad. I don't even know what's happening here today."

"It's a demonstration of a dummy missile and how the real thing is operated."

"Wow. I wish I could see it but Doctor Khan has sent all employees home."

They walked into a building and hurried down a small flight of stairs.

"This is a make-shift ground floor. We've had to cut the actual thing into half," the scientist explained. "The control room had to be set up here. Some superstition Doctor Khan believes in."

"So the ceiling must be false."

"Oh, yes. It's made of plywood. Good god, is that the time? Forgive me, ma'am, but I have to leave. *Khuda Hafiz.*"

"*Khuda Hafiz.*"

Varsha surveyed the controls in front of her. There were almost a hundred of them. From the glass window, she saw a party approaching. All of them went into the room above. One person came down to the control room. He was wearing a white lab coat.

"*Assalaam Waleiqum.* I am Doctor Afzal Khan. I run the Laboratories. You must be Salma Karim Afridi, the ISI lady who has helped us out."

"Yes, sir."

"It's nice to meet you. If you'll excuse me, I must go and have a cup of tea with the brass. I'll send somebody with something for you as well. We may take some time, so if you wish to sit upstairs, feel free to do so."

"Thank you, sir."

He moved to the control board, punched a few numbers on a pad and went off. A screen mounted on the panel said 'ACTIVATED AND AWAITING LAUNCH'.

Five minutes later, Atif and Iyer arrived, the latter wheeling a dustbin.

"You good, Varsha?" asked Atif.

"Never better. Ready?"

"What do we do?" asked Iyer.

"Atif, break open a bit of the plywood and place explosives there. Iyer, you and I will go through that door over there. The one which says 'Restricted Access'. I have a feeling that the missiles are behind It."

Atif quickly removed the plywood and started placing the IEDs and dynamite sticks. Iyer and Varsha ran through the passageway. They ran down two flights of stairs and were confronted by a door. Iyer broke it open and in front of them stood two enormous missiles. The room was lit by a single yellow bulb. The wall had a small built-in computer which Iyer tried to start.

"Won't start. Password protected."

"Try punching in a few random ones."

Two minutes later, Iyer reported failure.

"The computers are programmed differently. I don't think they needed to copy an IARDC system program for their computers."

"Okay. Let's see. What is the current status of the missiles?"

"The screen above them says 'ACTIVATED AND AWAITING LAUNCH'."

"To hell with the computer! Doctor Amanullah said that there is a panel fitted in the base of the missiles."

Iyer felt a wedge as he ran his hand over the base.

"Varsha, there's something here. I need some light."

She passed him a torch and he squeezed himself under the platform on which the missile stood. He opened the panel and was met by another keypad.

"Varsha, it's the panel Amanullah was talking about. We need an eight-digit password."

"Hell! Wait. Khan had punched something on a pad in the control room. Try this. Zero-nine-nine-one-five-zero-one-one. Anything?"

"We're in. Why didn't you tell me this password for the computer?"

"You had to switch the computer on. The program password and the computer password would surely not have been the same. What does the screen say?"

"It has two options: Launch and Deactivate."

"Deactivate it."

"Obviously."

"Okay. Deactivate the other one too. I'm placing the explosives. How long till Khan and the others get back?"

"Another ten minutes."

Varsha fitted explosives with timers on them onto the missiles. They fitted a few explosives on the walls, one on the computer and two on the door. Out of curiosity, Iyer flipped a switch next to the computer on. A smooth mechanism uncovered the top of the room and a rope ladder about two feet short of the ground fell towards them. They could see the clear evening sky. Varsha had a sudden idea.

"Help me up!" she said.

Iyer put his hands together for her to stand on and she made her way up the ladder. She jumped out into the open, placed explosives on the corners of the sliding roof and jumped back down. They hurried back and fitted one more on the back of the door that led to the control room. As they closed the door, they noticed that Atif had disappeared and they heard footsteps coming down the staircase. Iyer opened the 'Restricted Access' door and hid behind it. Khan opened the door and smiled at Varsha.

"Sorry for having kept you waiting. Did those men bring you anything?"

"Yes, thank you."

"Good. We're ready for the launch then. Let me just make a quick check on those bad boys."

He pressed a button on the panel and the screen displayed the missiles, adorned with explosives.

"What the hell is that?" Khan slammed his fist on the panel.

Khan took a moment to realise that there seemed to be an extra bit of light in the room. Varsha and Iyer had forgotten to flip the switch and close the roof! Varsha was taken aback by the sudden appearance of the room she had been hardly a minute back and before she could recover from the shock, Khan had grabbed her by the throat.

"What did you do, you witch?!" he sounded mad.

Varsha was gasping for breath and struggled but Khan, despite his small size, was strong. A moment later, the scientist fell down unconscious. Iyer had hit him on the head with a fire extinguisher. Atif came out from under the panel system.

"Are you okay?" he asked.

"No. I was nearly strangled. Of course I'm not okay!"

"Iyer, check for other cameras!" Atif commanded as he helped Varsha into a chair.

"No others," he said as soon as he had finished looking.

"Okay. Varsha, I'm going to destroy the camera. Iyer, try to wipe the footage."

Atif hurried to the underground room and fired shots at the camera. Satisfied, he hurried back.

"Atif, footage wiped."

"Good. Get the body out of the bin."

Just then, they heard a voice from one of the speakers.

"What's taking so long, Doctor Khan?"

Atif recognised the voice as that of the Prime Minister of Pakistan, Balqis Bilal.

"A few more minutes, madam," he said over the intercom in what was a passable imitation of Khan's voice.

Iyer pulled out the body of the real Salma Karim Afridi from the bin and placed it on the floor.

"Atif, shouldn't she be wearing my clothes? Just in case," Varsha pointed out. "You'll find a shirt and a pair of jeans in my purse. Pass them over and then turn around."

While Varsha changed, Atif and Iyer placed explosives on the bodies of Karim and Khan.

"We're good to go, Varsha. Ready yet?"

"Yup!"

Atif pulled out a satellite phone from his pocket and dialled.

"Gurpreet, blow the cars. Tell Sinha and Vir to bring the van to the rendezvous. We're leaving."

"All okay at your end?"

"Yes."

They pulled out their pistols. Atif and Iyer both held remotes in their hands and Varsha looked at her watch.

"Two minutes to the blast. Where's the exit?'"

"Follow me," said Atif.

He pulled a huge hammer out of his bag and hit out at the wall. Within thirty seconds, he had broken a large part of it. He quickly smashed a bit more of it and turned around to the other two.

"Let's go!"

They stepped out into the sun and ran towards the fence. A moment later, there was a series of blasts as a large number of cars blew up. A speeding van appeared out of nowhere and screeched to a stop in front of the trio. They hopped in and the van drove straight to the fence, broke through it, turned and halted on the road. Atif and Iyer immediately detonated the explosives. The room with a hole in the wall was set alight by the explosion. The panel sparked and blew up. A few moments later, the room with the VIPs blew up. Burning bodies flew out of the windows. A few moments later, there was a humongous explosion. The van's windows and windscreens shattered. The team looked up and saw pieces of the metal flying out of the missile hold. The team heard scrambling outside the van. Atif cautiously opened the door.

"It's us. Open the goddamn door," said Gurpreet impatiently.

"It's destroyed?" asked Akash eagerly.

"Well, you don't really see anything taking off from that place, do you?" Varsha was rather generous with the sarcasm.

"Don't bite my head off about it! General question. Where to now?"

"Home. Our job here is done. Sinha, drive as fast as you can!" commanded Gurpreet.

The sun had started to set as the seven R&AW officers drove off towards Sialkot.

**

19

THE FINAL ACT

MAY 11TH 1990
OFFICE OF THE SECRETARY (RESEARCH), SOUTH BLOCK
NEW DELHI, INDIA

"Thank you. Yes, we'll make an enquiry."

Thapar placed the receiver in its slot and mopped his sweaty forehead. He swore loudly when it ran again.

"Nikhil Thapar here."

"Nikhil, Sahni speaking."

"Good Evening, sir."

"Hi. What's this I'm hearing about Kahuta?"

"There has been a blast there, sir."

"Nikhil, do you take me to be a fool? Come to my place. Now!"

Thapar quickly knotted his tie and brushed his hair. He pulled on his blazer and walked out of the office, slamming the door shut. His driver had fallen asleep in his seat, just as he did whenever Thapar was late. He woke up when the car door slammed.

"Sanjay, 7 RCR."

The Ambassador sped through the empty roads of Delhi and drove into 7, Race Course Road in no time. Sahni was sitting on the lawn, smoking his pipe.

"Good Evening, sir."

"Nikhil, hi. Sit."

"Thank you, sir."

"Kahuta. Explain."

"It was a simple operation, sir. My team went there and did their job!"

"I'm sure they did. No wonder four of Pakistan's most prominent political and military leaders are dead! Along with the boss of the Kahuta Research Laboratories and three other people!"

"Sir, collateral damage."

"Nikhil, let's face facts. We are going to face a lot of flak for this stuff. Have you given any thought to what happens if anyone from your team is captured?"

"Sir, would you rather have Kashmir face a nuclear strike? I assure you that we won't face any flak. You did not sign any document about this operation. I didn't sanction it. These guys, until they enter the limits of India, are rogues. And as far as the question of their capture goes, we'll exercise plausible deniability if Pakistan manages to link them to us, which I doubt."

"This is a serious issue, Nikhil. Don't brush it off."

"I'm not brushing it off, sir. It's done. No point in crying over spilt milk. I assure you, nothing will be tied to us. In fact, if Pakistan says that they were struck by terror, you should reach out to them with an olive branch."

"I want a full account of the incident tomorrow morning. Where is your team right now?"

"I don't know. They left Kahuta at around five-thirty."

An attendant came up to Thapar, a phone on the tray.

"Sir, for you."

"Thanks," smiled Thapar. "Thapar here."

"Sir, Gurpreet speaking."

"Where are you?"

"Jammu. Flying out of here tomorrow morning."

"All good?"

"Yes, sir."

"Okay then. Good night."

Thapar kept the phone on a peg table and turned to Sahni.

"My team has reached Jammu, sir. They'll be back tomorrow morning. Do you want them to come for the briefing?"

"Okay. We'll have it here then. I'll be expecting you all by noon."

"Right, sir. Good night."

"Bye."

Thapar had reached the edge of the lawn when he heard Sahni call out.

"Nikhil!"

"Sir?"

"Well done."

Thapar smiled as he got into the Ambassador and drove off.

*

MAY 18TH 1990
SRINAGAR, INDIA

"Move fast. Come on!"

Three men in Army uniforms moved silently around the compound wall of a bungalow. Two policemen stood at the gates. The trio scaled the wall and dropped into the garden. They spotted an ajar side door. They opened it and entered the house. They made their way to the study. Someone was sitting at the desk inside. They opened fire at the figure. They quickly ran out of the study and rushed out of the side door. The sight outside made their jaws drop. Fifteen policemen were standing there, their SLRs pointed at the trio. They dropped the weapons and put their hands up. The sight of Maulana Omar Faisal standing in front of them shocked them even more. They were thrown into a police van and taken away.

In Badami Bagh Cantonment, Syed Mohammed Ali Hussain was pacing up and down his cell. He kept looking at his watch. The door of his cell flew open and he was dragged out. He was handcuffed, pushed into a jeep and driven off to the Corps Headquarters. He was brought before Lieutenant General Anwar.

"Hussain, what is the date today?"

"May 18th."

"Is there something special today?"

"Not that I know of."

"Do you know that Maulana Omar Faisal was attacked today?"

"Was he?"

"Indeed, he was."

"Did he survive?"

"Sorry to dash your hopes but he did."

"Faisal isn't my enemy. Our ideologies are different but our mission is the same."

"Facts contradict that. If he isn't your enemy, why did you have him kidnapped?"

"You shouldn't throw such allegations around."

"I'm not alleging it. We have a recording in which you've admitted that the kidnapping was your brainchild. And we also have the word of an officer of the Indian Army. And SP Ganjoo's confession."

"That audio is definitely doctored. And Baig is lying. And who the hell is Ganjoo?"

"I don't want this to be a long and arduous conversation, Hussain. I'll ask you once again: did you plan to murder Maulana Omar Faisal?"

"No."

"Are you sure?"

"Even if I did, I wouldn't tell you."

"I know that. But we have other ways of checking. For now, we can hand over the audio and also present the confessions of the men who carried out the attack."

"They confessed?"

"C'mon, Hussain. You didn't really expect them to keep quiet, did you? They're poor chaps who've got families. If they agree to testify against you, their families will be safe. And we have enough to put you away for life at the minimum. I'll keep my fingers crossed and hope that the judge sees you for who you are and sentences you to death."

"You're bluffing. You just want me to talk."

"Maybe."

Anwar picked up the telephone on his table.

"Take him away."

"You can't hold me forever. You'll have to hand me over to the police. I'll get the best lawyers in this country to fight my case."

"What a hypocrite you are! You criticise this country, raise militant groups to attack it, insult its Flag and then take help from its own people to get out of trouble."

"I'm a senior citizen. I'll ask to be put under house arrest. You people will just watch. You know as well as I do that all India can do is cry and complain."

"That's the political way of doing things. I am an army officer. There are a lot of things I can do which the government won't know about. And I hope you are put under house arrest. Makes perfect sense. Don't they fatten the goat before slaughtering it? Think of yourself in that context," Anwar laughed.

Hussain looked a little disturbed. Anwar was confident that he had unsettled him. There was a knock on the door.

"Come in."

Some men walked in and lifted Hussain from his seat. As they reached the door, Anwar spoke.

"Hussain, congratulations. We're releasing you into the custody of the Jammu and Kashmir Police."

Hussain smiled rather sinisterly as he was pulled away. He was held tightly by two burly policemen and marched to the car.

"How are you, Khanna?" Hussain laughed.

"Let's go. You two, hold on to him," DSP Khanna pointed at Hussain as the ignition in his Gypsy was turned on.

The two vehicles moved quickly through the maze of roads. As they turned around a particular blind turn, a white Maruti van came into sight. A second later, there was a loud boom and a flash of light, followed by a screech of tyres and a crash. The Gypsy rammed into a tree. Grabbing a minor window of opportunity, Hussain successfully freed himself from the now-loose grip of his captors and jumped out. One of the policemen grabbed his *kurta* but it tore off. The policeman threw the piece of cloth to the ground and followed Hussain. The Separatist leader slipped and went rolling down a grassy slope. The policeman kneeled down and waited for Hussain to get up and run. Hussain looked over his shoulder as soon as he reached the end of the slope and ran for it. He heard a shot and saw the bullet strike a tree in front of him. He hardly had any time to rejoice as the next bullet pierced him in the butt. He fell down, grabbing hold of the fine grass as blood poured out of the wound. A minute later, he was hauled back to the Gypsy.

"Tie this rascal up!" ordered Khanna.

His face had lots of small cuts and a shard of glass was lodged in his forearm.

"Move it!"

The van was burning as the two vehicles went past it. The windows and windscreens were almost non-existent. On the dashboard lay a severed hand. Human remains were strewn all over the wreck and had spilt on to the road.

"Move once again and I'll shoot you dead. I mean it," Khanna warned the howling Hussain. "And stop being a sissy!"

At Crime Branch, a doctor cleaned up Hussain's bullet wound. Khanna was also patched up along with his driver.

"Watch out. The man is crazy. Put two constables inside his cell. And they must be alert," the doctor told Khanna.

Five days later, the Jammu and Kashmir High Court accepted Hussain's request to be put under house arrest. The establishment was stunned. The Separatists and their supporters were ecstatic. Hussain was cheered by small crowds all the way to his residence.

"*Hum kya chahte?*" he yelled from the balcony of his home in Hyderpora.

"*Azadi!*" came the response from the crowd below.

*

MAY 27TH 1990
HUSSAIN MANSION, HYDERPORA
SRINAGAR, INDIA

"Hussain *sahib*, the workers have to repair the windows and ledges outside your study. Shall I let them?"

"Okay. I have finished my meetings for today. But tell them to make as little noise as possible."

Repairs and cleaning had been going on for the last couple of days. Hussain had been adamant that his study and the top of the house not be touched until the last day of repairs. Media personnel were at the gates of the bungalow with their cameras and mikes. The police *bandobast* was water-tight. Each repairman and cleaner was searched before he got to work. On the roof, a chair-and-pulley arrangement was fixed. It was lowered down to the study window. Hussain sat at his desk, reading.

"*Assalaam Waleiqum*, Hussain *sahib*," said the workers.

"*Waleiqum Assalaam*. Work properly," Hussain continued reading, not even looking up.

Hussain got up at about five o'clock, half an hour before his evening walk, and went to fetch a book from his library upstairs. He heard the hammering of nails as he walked up the stone steps.

"Pipe down, you bloody fools!" he shouted.

"Apologies, *jenab*," came a voice through the open window.

He walked past the numerous shelves of books, wondering about which one to pick next.

"Be careful. That thing is made from teak wood that cost more than you'll earn in your entire life," he snarled at a man who was lifting a bookcase.

He selected three books from the last row of shelves and made his way back to the staircase. As he was about to step on to the first step, the carpet slipped from under his feet. The last thing Hussain saw was a pair of gun-metal grey eyes glinting before his head smashed into one of the steps and he fell down the narrow staircase. He was sprawled out on the bottom. He had rolled over on his way down. The worker in the room yelled for help.

"Hussain *sahib* has fallen down the stairs. Call an ambulance!"

The ambulance took an hour to arrive. By then, the family doctor had already declared Hussain dead. The worker from the library helped lift Hussain's stretcher and take it to the ambulance. The police officer in charge came to him a minute later.

"What happened?"

"Hussain *sahib* took some books and was about to go down the staircase when he slipped and fell down the stairs," the man wiped his tears.

"Relax. Go over there, give your statement to the constable and leave."

The constable was recording the statements of all the other workers. The man quickly gave his statement and left.

"We did it, buddy," Baig looked up at the clear sky, a lump in his throat as he walked to the rickshaw stand. "We did it. Operation Blazing Snow is a success!"

***

EPILOGUE

Militancy in Kashmir grew steadily in the 90s. It hit its peak in 1995-96. Militants started to hit schools and government offices. People were given a choice: stop working for the government or die. An entire generation went to rot. Children were doing drugs. In 1996, Assembly Elections were held in the state after six years of Governor's Rule. Farhad Ahmed was re-elected as Chief Minister. Around the same time, a lot of militants started to surrender and join the Ikhwanis. And as they were well aware of the militant network, they turned out to be quite resourceful. Later on, the Separatists, along with the Hizbul Mujahideen, started to hunt the Ikhwani leaders down one-by-one. It led to an unprecedented meltdown and the Ikhwani network collapsed, leaving only small groups of informers. In 1998, the Indian Amy launched OPERATION SADBHAVANA, aimed at building a good rapport with the locals and also to bring the Valley back to its feet. Since the turn of the millennium, insurgency in the Valley has subsided considerably, with leaders opting to hold talk rather than wield an AK-47. However, there have been major skirmishes in the last sixteen years. Separatists continue to incite people in the Valley and Pakistan continues to train them. Tourism came to a sudden halt in 1989 but has picked up again, with millions flocking to explore Kashmir every year. The Valley was devastated in the 2014 floods. People lost everything. The handicraft industry and apple crops were two of the worst-hit. The Indian Armed Forces, with assistance from local Kashmiri youth, carried out extensive rescue operations across the state under 'OPERATION MEGH RAHAT' even as the State Government under Umar Ahmed floundered. The current situation is somewhat rocky but is a vast improvement from the haunting 90s.

Maulana Omar Faisal floated the Awami Council in 1993 after withdrawing his Moderates faction from the Hardliner-dominated APAKC. He is currently a Member of Parliament in the Lok Sabha.

Shehnaaz Baig divorced Randeep Singh in 1990 and is currently the Vice Chancellor of Delhi University.

Vikrant Pratap retired as a Lieutenant General in 2011.

Neil Kapoor is a serving Brigadier and is currently posted in Ladakh.

Nikhil Thapar was killed by militants in Srinagar while serving as a security advisor to the Governor of Jammu and Kashmir during the 1996 Assembly Elections.

Samir Ali took premature retirement from the IPS in 2000 and is a successful screenwriter for films.

Gurpreet Singh retired as a Major General in 2015.

Varsha Menon left the R&AW in 1990 and has been a travel and food journalist for the last twenty-six years.

Akash Mehra left the R&AW IN 1992 and worked in various firms. In 1999, he founded a company 'Chroma Key Studios', which specialises in visual and special effects for films and video games.

Liaquat Khaleel Baig is a serving Lieutenant General. Since his stint in the R&AW ended, he has served in Siachen and the Andaman & Nicobar Islands, among various other locations. He was awarded the Ashoka Chakra for Counter-Insurgency Operations while commanding a battalion in the Valley in 2000. He is currently posted in Sri Ganganagar, Rajasthan.

**

ACKNOWLEDGEMENTS

Mamma-Papa. I cannot possibly thank them enough. Dedicating OPERATION BLAZING SNOW to them is a very small way of saying thank you. I remember the time when Papa used to tell my sister and me a story before saying 'good night'. More often than not, he ended up telling us two or three of them. And it didn't matter how tired he was after work. It's been almost ten years since the last story, Papa. You may have to tell us one soon. Mamma was the one who put up with the constant complaints my sister and I had about the other. She was the negotiator between the two hostile parties. While we missed Papa a lot when he was out, Mamma took on both roles successfully. My sister and I would never have picked up a book and developed a habit of reading had it not been for our parents. Had they not pushed us to read, you wouldn't be reading this page. Mamma-Papa, I know that I don't say it a lot but I love both of you very much and am proud to be your son.

My sister Mriganka and my friend Moey, both of whom are basically the same person. She was the only person who was critical of my work and even me told when she didn't like a story I was writing. Her frankness made me improve my work. Thanks, Mriganka! Lots of love. Now for the little one, Champagne. A most amazing person who hasn't read a word of what I have written. Thank you for being who you are, Champagne. You're a wonder! Loads of love from Varun *dada*.

My friends: Nikhil, Gurpreet, Varsha, Akash, among a whole bunch of others. My victims when I wrote nonsensical stuff and forced them to read it. Thanks for sticking by me. All of you are an amazing bunch of people.

Relatives and friends and colleagues of my parents who read the pieces of work that I have put up on the Internet. Thank you for all that you said about my writing.

I would like to thank my father's *sahayaks*/buddies who are all like older brothers to me. They have played a significant part in making me a better person. Thank you, *bhaiyas*!

Clichéd as it may sound, I want to thank the personnel of the Defence Services and Central Armed Police Forces of India for the incredible work they do. In particular, the Indian Army, which has been a huge inspiration and a constant in my sixteen years of existence. Thank you!

All the writers whose work I read as I grew up. JK Rowling and her stunning Harry Potter books, Sir PG Wodehouse with his amazing humour, Ruskin Bond for his variety of stories, Chris Kuzneski and his thrillers, Roald Dahl for all of his stories, Sir Arthur Conan Doyle for the most amazing detective known to mankind, Enid Blyton for the numerous series', Bill Watterson for Calvin & Hobbes, René Goscinny and Albert Uderzo for Asterix, Hergé for Tintin, Hank Ketcham for Dennis the Menace, DC Thompson & Co. Ltd. for Commando and all the non-fiction writers whose work interested me. You were and continue to remain inspirations. Your amazing work kept me hooked to books and comics.

My notebooks, pens and laptop, for staying where you were left and remaining in the same state as you were left.

And thank you! Thank you for reading OPERATION BLAZING SNOW!

***